Praise for Michael Frost Beckner
&
SPY GAME

"Pass the popcorn!"
—*Amazon Editors' Pick*, Vanessa Cronin, Sr. Editor

"Brilliantly executed...First-class spy novels with a smart, gritty atmosphere."
—Charles Cumming, *New York Times & Sunday Times Best-selling Author of KENNEDY 35* and *BOX 88*

"A thinking man's thriller... A real adrenaline blast... I loved it!"
—Robert Redford

"There's nobody quite like Beckner. Cerebral and unvarnished...with dialogue so sharp it's like dancing on hot coals. You'll swallow this book whole."
—I.S. Berry, *Edgar winning Author of THE PEACOCK AND THE SPARROW, A New Yorker & NPR Best Book of the Year*

"Michael Frost Beckner serves up a judicious blend of showy action, political intrigue, ticking-clock suspense, and CIA one-upmanship for mainstream entertainment."
—*Variety*

"There is nothing like *The Aiken Trilogy*... Laced with absurdity & stylistically daring ... Beckner [is] a razzle-dazzle showman at the top of the thriller heap."
—Editor's Pick, *Publishers Weekly*

"Beckner is one of the most unabashedly duplicitous writers I've ever encountered ... Brilliant work."
—Stephen England, *Best-selling Author of the SHADOW WARRIOR Series*

"Michael Frost Beckner is the rarest of spy novelists, a beautiful and compelling writer who also has a mastery of tradecraft and a deep understanding of how espionage really works."
—Joe Weisberg, *former CIA Officer and EMMY Award-winning creator of The Americans*

ALSO BY MICHAEL FROST BECKNER

HITLER'S LOKI
Berlin Mesa

SPY GAME
The Aiken Trilogy
Muir's Gambit
Bishop's Endgame
Aiken in Check

KALEIDOSCOPE: A SPY GAME SERIAL
4th of July
Birthday
Halloween
Thanksgiving

A NATION DIVIDED
Volume I: From West Point to the Seven Days Battles
Volume II: From the Battle of Second Manassas to Chattanooga
Volume III: From the Battle of The Wilderness to Appomattox

Kaleidoscope

A Spy Game Serial

Part 4:

Thanksgiving

Michael Frost Beckner

MONTROSE STATION PRESS

Las Vegas
2025

Published in the United States Montrose Station Press LLC

ISBN 9798990351776 (paperback)
ISBN 9798990351769 (ebook)

Printed in the United States of America

Jacket Design & Illustrations by Andrew Frost Beckner

FIRST EDITION 2025

For Tracy Mercer
No better friend had the Kingstons

KALEIDOSCOPE:

THANKSGIVING

"To hear the sadness in things is a kind of listening, and it is nothing but the sweetest love."

—T. H. White, *The Once and Future King*

Prologue

THE EYE OF A tornado is a kaleidoscope.

April 11, 1965. A balmy Palm Sunday. The severe Midwest weather people paid attention to happened yesterday. Down along the Kansas-Missouri line. A little swing farther south into Central Arkansas. A few lives lost. Sad, but nothing to do with Indiana. Here, in Elkhart County, plans for Easter Week—

Kids: school vacation/egg hunt bunny baskets.

Parents: "I'll be needing a new dress and a hat for church."/"Guess I'd better mow the lawn before your folks and the cousins roll in."

—mostly all what's on people's minds when the first twister stabs from the sky at 3:20 pm. Until 9:00 am the following morning, ten F4/F5 tornados obliterate this north-middle section of the Hoosier State.

1,200 injured.

137 people dead.

1.217 billion dollars damage.

The worst hit is Dunlap. 6:32 pm. A double funnel separates. Plows on a cross the aluminum thick Midway Trailer Court. Kills ten. Plows a farm field. Then the two black cones coalesce into a single tornado, gurgitating metal beams, screws, siding, glass, creatures, fixtures and someone's hoarded books. (They found over two hundred in the days to come; out near where the Putnam homestead vanished.) This debris corkscrews inside the vortex. A lethal payload spiraling to 277 miles per hour.

Strikes Middlebury boom-like-a-bomb.

Rends to shards and shreds farms, homes, neighbor-hoods. An entire town blown apart in a black howl. Destruction so immense—

Families swept away, two church dinners, half the audience delighting to Julie Andrews Do-Re-Mi'ing The Sound of Music *sucked in theater seats right out the roof; "Elmer," the soldier from the Civil War monument ninety-nine years resting on his musket, transforms into a bronze missile and takes out the gas station.*

So thorough—

Underground fuel tanks erupt through blacktop in volcanos of fire. Wind-rowling flames ignite a mael-strom of burning paper, shed from the Town Hall ripped asunder.

Destruction so complete—

Grief/hopelessness/PTSD: All that's left survivors in-capable of sorting anything out of the phantasmagoric devastation.

Number of dead for Dunlap/Middlebury?

Maybe as low as fourteen. Maybe worse at twen-ty-three. Some diligent searchers—individuals with the guts to sort bits small as a finger curled around a blade of grass, an eyeball dangling in a pile of branches, a foot split lengthwise like an open book beneath a broken panel of corrugated fiberglass—tick on the putt-putt golf cards they use to log their discoveries:

~~Fourteen.~~ ~~Sixteen.~~ Twenty-three.

Twenty-six.

Thirty-one. Thirty-seven. Thirty-eight.

Forty.

Forty-seven years later, "14 to 40 Dead" remains the officially disagreed upon number of fatalities.

♛ ♛ ♛

WHEREAS A SINGLE INCIDENT of random bad luck met with miraculous grace gathers a net around unfathomable terror and draws it tightly; though remembered, re-marked, identified—albeit hardly known—the image of one family bitterly broken that day becomes, if not the moral (no, never that; no good versus evil enlightenment glimmers hopeful out of the random destructions of God), then, at least, that family becomes the emblem of the tragedy.

That family becomes its touchstone.

Becomes its face.

Here, the family DeGrange spins into fractured focus.

While no one would ever say Leo DeGrange had always been unlucky, no one ever argued he was all too smart. Survivor of one of the bloodiest battles of World War Two, he'd earned the right to be dumb, and good/bad luck is an equal opportunity finger of fate. Where business came into play, primarily the business of providing for his family, one Leo-dumb decision shook hands with bad luck, one Tuesday night that March; catapulted the DeGranges into history.

A traveling salesman by trade—and stop your mind where it's wearing a path to the farmer's wife or daughter; sure, there are plenty of stories about the lustful travelling man fornicating his way through town/county/state; Leo's virtue was unbudge-able—Leo DeGrange was an Iwo Jima landing beach crap-pants-teenage-boot to Mount Suribachi leather-neck'd-soul-holed-old-man five days later, twenty years hence door-to-door'ing ("Ne'er-mind the limp, ma'am, it don't bother me none") all those goods and gadgets that eased the Silent Generation housewife's labor and educated their rabbit test bunny-boom of offspring. And whether he had a willing opportunity (and there were plenty), Leo never stuck a foot in a door that was fol-lowed by step into a bedroom. Might have been luck-ier if he bedded a'one or a'two or a whole lot more of them—the situation his virtue puts him in. But alas, Leo DeGrange was a faithful husband. Altar to the grave.

Well, headstone at any rate; they never found the body, so no one did any digging.

Leo DeGrange copulated at home where he proved more concupiscent than any drummer on the road. Just without the randy roadman's number one precaution.

Condoms.

Folks say each time an unhappy, no-sale face slammed a door in Leo DeGrange's kisser, the more comfort he sought kissing his wife, and the more merry faces she added round their kitchen table. Moral quib-bles be damned, not sowing any oats—and his wilder than most—Leo ended up up to his nostrils drowning in weeds.

A man on the road also precautions himself with a budget. Leo did. For the road but not for home. One of everything he sells, he's gifted to his family. On cred-

it. Too late, Leo realizes no amount of brushes, vacuums, or sewing machines; encyclopedias, magazines, will ever translate into enough income to support the wife, mother-in-law, and ten growing children a commercial traveler has no business having. No electric juicers; home barber kits; no record-music subscriptions and the turntable go-withs; no summer-crate fruit and field corn bushel barrel will save Leo DeGrange from loan-drowning in his Servicemen Readjustment Act too small at any rate subdivision home.

Still safe yet—he doesn't live in Indiana—a late knock on his door, Shrove Tuesday (another pancake night for the hungry family now living every day on penny-supper flapjacks), snares Leo into the old Putnam homestead he occupies ten days into Lent. Before that most brutal of Palm Sundays.

Ash Wednesday, Leo quits Owensboro, Kentucky, to take a shot at Dunlap, Indiana. Proud/bemused owner of the Putnam homestead. By the time Leo DeGrange arrives at the dilapidated ramshackle, he admits to himself his decision at the knock-knock on his door to fall for whatever too good to be true pitch staked him from his porch.

That's where dumb comes in. Saw the fool move. Made it, anyway.

"Sir, I take it you're a veteran."

"True 'nuf."

"Then this is your lucky night. I'm Ernst P. Gladstone. Plymouth Land and Soldiers Trust, see? 'Title Company,' tacked to the end, just to be formal. Out of our nation's capital, no less. Fixing up the kit of every GI vet gone upside down on his GI Loan. Don't mind my impertinence, bud, but I can see you're carryin' around a little piece a'the war, way you favor that good leg. M'I right, or m'I right? Krauts?"

"T'other."

Gladstone pulled his sleeve. A jagged scar, looking fresh healed. Kind you get on a farmer's fence going after a goat or outrunning a shotgun. "Jap bayonet."

Leo forced his imagination to play along.

"As a P-L-S-T'n'T Authorized Agent, I am under government authority to sell no-interest deeds to vacated homestead properties. Originally farmed under the Homestead Act. 1862. Government property of the government, by the government, for the government to take care of its own who've—no fault *a'their* own—fallen to hard times."

"You're from the government, y'say?"

"Their certified agent. Yessir. 'Me.' I'm here t'help."

The wink. The smile. The hand-shook stupidity meeting the worst luck imaginable.

Leo plucks a weed. Gives it a chew. Could be worse. The pitch was mostly true. Same government would have offered any American, Leo included, this same Putnam property for one-quarter the price. For the asking. If he'd a'known to ask. For that matter, could a'cost Leo zero if he'd just shut his eyes, his mouth, and shut the door.

The Putnam homestead: one of dozens of cast-offs in Indiana alone; turkeys useless for farming crops, or for that matter, turkeys to any profit, but Leo DeGrange is a determined man. Determined to turn his life around and do well by his family. Especially since mouth-to-feed number eleven made the news flash on the road trip up.

Hands on his hips. Weed-stalk dancing between his teeth. Leo DeGrange stares at the Putnam homestead. A canted and ungainly six-room/double-loft cabin (or barn, depending on whether you're viewing north-south with the windows or east-west with the rolling door) on a four-acre weed lot, same distance plus change to the Midway Trailer Court. Leo convinces himself that, with a little luck and a lot of elbow grease, and sweat, and, might as well say it, devilish hard work, there's yet enough life left in this dirt to provide for his ever-expanding brood better than he had it in Kentucky.

New goal: self-sufficient/door-shut in Dunlap.

All he needs. When you got all of nothing else, it better be. Leo's dream. For the making. And damn it all to hell if he ever ding-dongs another doorbell.

♔ ♔ ♔

FULL CIRCLE BACK to that balmy Indiana Palm Sunday.

Spit distance from those Midway trailers.

The wife— "Eating for two, now, dear;" Leo thanks the Lord for that. Asks thanks for the pork chops. Seven for the thirteen of them (plus a week of bones for the dog). Divided big part/little part the way the DeGrange crew sit. Tall-next-to-small-next-to-tall-to-small and so forth around the table. He's grateful. You can stretch a dollar here in Dunlap and already it's not-no-more penny pancakes for us and he's looking forward to getting some callouses on the inside of his prayer-folded hands. Match their door-worn knuckles.

He thanks the Lord for his family.

Includes his mother-in-law.

All of them are grateful, hand-clasped around the two dinner tables pushed together in the main room on this wholly unholy spring day, that 6:32 pm moment when the tornado touches down.

Splits double.

Rips the shape of the cross through the trailer park to meet side-by-side, rotating round each other like dervishes. They enter the field where—6:33—the larger of the two sidetracks south. There exist some photos of this. Shuffle them fast enough: that sidetrack looks awful-lot-like a hound going from scent to sight, taking right off for the Putnam homestead like it means to kill it. The structure disintegrates. The fat funnel sucks the entire place—its thirteen occupants (plus one on the way), its milk cow, chicken coop, its goats and its dog—into its cone.

Up-up-and-away. Gone.

Not having made more than a hand-wave acquaintance with any of the wrecked survivors of the trailer park, having been to church less times than Leo could count on his thumb, in the disaster's aftermath, no one remembers the DeGrange family came to Indiana at all.

♛ ♛ ♛

Four days pass. Dinnertime, April 15, 1965. A young girl somnambulates into Goshen's Red Cross rescue center. Set up in the parish hall of the undamaged Lutheran church. For those keeping track, it's Maundy Thursday. Night when Christ—loaf of bread/cup/covenant, the washing of the feet—made something meaningful in the cleaning of wounded and wounds, and those in this place not wounded enough for a hospital bed, but bad off enough to be there on cots; even though not a'one is remembering Jesus mysteries, all are invisibly and perfectly united in benumbed horror by this:

Just as I have loved you, you also should love one another.

Dirty. Pale-skinned. Not a stitch of clothing, oh-my. Her mouth agape, the young girl is unable to speak. She clutches a dog collar. Holds it out like a sort of talisman and her vacant eyes roll tears without sobs. Without sniffles. Down her high and bruised, her scraped and bloodied cheeks. The temporary metal ring/cardboard-center dog tag will identify her not as Beaumont (Owensboro tax-numbered/rabies-vaccinated) Lic. #76-3014, but as the single survivor of the family DeGrange.

Questions ring. She doesn't say a word. Stares at nothing, or, maybe, a metaphysical everything. Eyes like distant stars. Dark blue. Diamond cerulean crypts.

A nurse wraps the blue-eyed girl in a blanket. A volunteer fireman offers her a paper cup of coffee. She takes the coffee. Remembers thankfulness—almost—the last thought she'd had before she hadn't thought another.

Wrapped in the blanket, she sits with the coffee. With the dog collar. Takes a sip. Loses grip on the cup. Scalds her lap and doesn't notice. Takes unconsciousness, which suits her best.

Six days, a coma holds onto the mystery of how she has arrived almost three miles southeast from Dunlap. The place where the dog license indicates Beaumont's master recently relocated. Where his dog recently frolicked. No one knows for sure which DeGrange this girl is, but when she awakens, after she drinks water, and when she speaks, she confirms what others have guessed.

The girl is Doris DeGrange. She is fourteen years of age and, most massively, an orphan.

The press dubs Doris "Indiana's Easter Miracle." Third oldest of Leo and Harriet DeGrange's children, Doris has no memory of how she got from her dinner table—one of those two pushed together that dominated the DeGrange homestead its few short days—to the children's ward of the hospital in Fort Wayne. After Leo amen'd his pork chop blessing, a wind, baying like one thousand hounds, slammed all sides of their stupid/unlucky Putnam cast-off all at once.

"I was holding Beaumont. Holding his collar. Then I sipped coffee. Then I was here. He had the front of my sweater in his bite—I remember that. The force of his jaws in the tug on the wool. It was my favorite red one. Sweater. Has anyone found my dog? Anyone found Beaumont?"

♔ ♔ ♔

IN 1965, IN GOSHEN, INDIANA, Doris DeGrange is the kaleidoscope image walking out of a tornado's funnel; five years later, she walks down the aisle of the mossed-stone family chapel at Foxtail Farm in Hollywood, Maryland. Joins Silas Kingston at the family altar. Joins Silas Kingston in marriage. A family ceremony. Private; no DeGranges left. Only Kingstons.

One exception. Silas Kingston's boss, his great mentor, James Jesus Angleton. ARTIFICE in his OSS days. The Associate Deputy Director of Operations for Counterintelligence, or, "The Ghost" at CIA, who, having introduced Silas to Doris, has given the bold orphan away to matrimony.

Good luck and smart, a dream/hope/aspiration of new family all her own.

The orphan bride's wedding bouquet is complex and beautiful. Red river lilies with Angleton's prized dendrobium orchids engulf Doris's fists. Orchids trail from Doris's hair to linger down her back in lengths of yellow-hued Mexican vanilla orchid vine: the golden garlands of a blushing queen.

As a wedding gift, Angleton presents the married couple a pair of round matched sorcerer mirrors.

Silas puzzles their shape. "Unusual, sir."

Angleton lifts one of the round glasses from its tissued nest. "Yes. These reverse convex optics" —he indicates twenty-four circular nodes ringing the circumference— "draw light from the entire room and throw it around to magical effect. A sixteenth century Italian design—though these are eighteenth century Irish—considered excellent glasses for scrying."

"Which is...?" Silas, again. "What?"

"They're lovely, Jim. Thank you." Doris—came to Angleton's attention at Barnard College from which he whirlwinded her into Yale—beams. To her new husband she says, "Scrying is the art of divining messages; receiving visions by gazing into a looking glass."

"'Mirror, mirror, on the wall' and all that?"

"Yes, my love. The Evil Queen is scrying."

Angleton, who couldn't recruit her but loves her like a daughter, blesses Doris with a wink. "These were mine. From my younger days. I had them first at Malvern, in Worcestershire, England, before our Yale. In my chamber, one hung in front, one behind my desk. Where I edited the Furioso.*"*

"It's not my Yale." Doris demurs demure. "I only completed a year."

Silas takes her hand. "You'll finish when we're back."

Doris yearns. Knows this won't come true.

Angleton hasn't heard. "'These with a thousand small deliberations/Protract the profit of their chilled delirium,/Excite the membrane, when the sense has cooled—'"

Not an easy man to follow, the bridegroom and bride share an awkward glance.

"'With pungent sauces, multiply variety/In a wilderness of mirrors. What will the spider do/suspend its operations, will the weevil/ Delay?'"

Silas takes the bait. "Shakespeare?"

"T.S. Eliot." Angleton verifies with a nod, much to himself. Serious. Reflective. Looks into the mirror, flat in his hands. Held like a paten. His face in the center, scrying, perhaps from the sorcerer mirror—

A cutting of photographs.

Trapezoids and triangles onto the bed.

Scattered.

Spread.

Separated.

—Silas and Doris see themselves captured along the edges in reverse optics. Human images met and flung in all matter of angles; flung and scattered with the light.

"He was a friend—Eliot was." The CIA spook looks at the pair. "Remember your friends. Remember, most of all and through it all, you two came first together as friends." Deeper meaning in Angleton's expression. Earnest, unspoken, more than Silas can divine, and more that Doris knows. Angleton spreads arms, black-sleeved, bird-bone wings without feathers, and clutches them. "Friendship. Most important for a marriage."

♕♕♕

NO TIME FOR A HONEYMOON. Doris asks if they might bring Beaumont—the Welsh Terrier Silas has given her that summer—with them to Moscow. She knows they cannot; Silas soothes her; his parents will care for Beaumont in their absence.

Moscow happens.

When they return, Michael swaddled, bubbling/cooing in his mother's arms, Silas takes the dog—bounding and jumping, exuberant at the sight of them—to the back acreage. From the stone Sylvanus Bench, he throws a tennis ball. They play to the long side of two hours. He ponders what Doris admitted in the night.

"In 1904, a thunderstorm gathered over Tula. The blackest storm anyone had ever seen. As it approached the Moscow suburbs, it split into three tornado funnels."

When Silas deems her animal delirious, peak enjoyment/luxuriant exhaustion, deems his own misery, building inside his chest to a grief-stricken scream that if loosed, would only frighten the animal—

My youth has failed me; I am Eliot's Gerontion; his little old man—

"I that was near your heart was removed therefrom
To lose beauty in terror, terror in inquisition."

—victim to Angleton's warped mirrors; love the instrument of torture, confessing faith as sin.

He cups the dog's muzzle. Warms its heart with gentle words of praise.

Silas knows of all the things he has done and will do, things which might send him to hell, what he will do now guarantees the journey. And why? Because as enraged as Doris's unapologetic betrayal makes him, he cannot face the prospect of eternity without a surety that he will be eternally at her side. She is going to Hell and so, he will go there too.

He presses the other muzzle. Understands that, unlike Kolya's gun Silas pressed to the back of MI6 agent Evander Lott's head—knees down/run down in a steam-blown Moscow alley—what he chooses to do now is unjust.

It is evil. Pure and large writ.

Because he is young and foolish in youth, he is mistaken; in his torment, he cannot see the devil at his most triumphant.

Silas looks out. Eyes lensed with emotion. The barren of Turkey's Swan Song, wet and wavered by his tears. The truth of all the evil buried beneath that dirt by generations of unapologetic Kingstons speaks to him.

The truth of the Kingston legacy.

He fires his pistol.

After Beaumont dies, Silas Kingston never allows another dog inside the gates of Foxtail Farm. Like all his

*ancestors before him who sat this Sylvanus stone seat,
he has made the devil's work his pact with God.*

Fall

1.

O N NOVEMBER 1, 2012, between the hours of two and three in the morning, inside Room 206 of the Old Carriage House Hotel, Roman Sayadov buttoned his black silk shirt. He tucked it into his waistline. He admired the curve of Lynn's shoulder. The tousle of her auburn hair across it, sheening in the bar of rectangular light that split the darkness from the half-open bathroom door at his back. Beauty—private and absolute; for this moment, his—flowed in lazy twists over and off her upturned, unblemished shoulder. Her body, so muscular and electric scant hours before, soft and flushed with inner heat, slack in sleep.

Trusting. Vulnerable.

He mistook the moisture on the visible cheek of her half-turned face as residual glow of their surprising (unsurprised?)—very much wished-for, granted, and claimed—frenzied encounter. Her initial surrender. A powerful statement to his manhood. Followed by her overtaking him with a Halloween-suitable mania of unleashed lust. Their second time. (Of many more to come?) He hoped. He smiled. "You're quite a woman, Layla Kingsbury."

His lips found her lips. Cool. Cushioned soft. A spark of response. A quiver Roman mistook for pleasure emanated from Lynn Kingston in sleep. Equal, in his mind alone, to the honest pleasure kissing "Layla" returned to him.

He left the room, careful not to wake her. The urge to see her again dominated thoughts of the day ahead. Dominated his day with thoughts of Layla throughout.

DREAM DIALOGUE. Mindscape mathematics. Memories oscillate; bits of color mirror-image.

Chipped-polish, teenage toes. Curled in sand and seashell muck.

Grown-Lynn toes, unpolished. Curled in sand and seashell muck.

Emotions are light and they strobe.

Chipped-polish-teenage (risk-rush excitement; cheap-maturity guilt).

No-polish-adult (shame; compassion; guilt; fire-stoked courage).

Faster now. Turned and falling. Turned, and coming together, bind in pattern.

Chipped toenails: needy desire; incautious bravery—feelings ingurgitated by the oozing muck of time—horror; resolve: toenails unchipped.

Oozing muck locks into a "present."

I am there.

There is here: looking up from teenage toes, peering up from the tree trunk drift log, sapwood sun-bleached white and wind/sand-fuzzed as Silas-still-Dad demon-strates—

"Put your lips like this. On the edge. Blow across the top."

I am thirteen. (Nothing—my life/my me-I-am—has yet to happen; I want it badly.) Dad teaches me to whistle on his beer bottle. I try. Get it right away. "May I have a sip?"

(I want it badly.)

"Just one. One sip."

"Silas!" Mom stops. Hovers over the pit. Stops layering the wet, knotted wrack we've pulled from the rocks, pulled over the fire stones and pulled over the embers. "Stop. Don't give her beer. Honestly."

"Doris, I said, 'one sip.'"

Seaweed sizzles.

"It's just one sip, Mom!"

"Alright. Just. One." Slaps more seaweed. Sizzle on the stones.

But all night, after my first sip, I sip-sip-sip every time Dad puts his bottle down.

Silas sees. Silas knows. His laughing eyes. (Mocking me?)

I defy him and I finish his next bottle—but, oh, he wasn't looking at me at all; he's watching Michael and Hal—

"Careful, boys, on those stairs!"

—dangerous beach stairs down with the green Army box. The Army mortar.

It's the last clam bake we always do—it's Halloween always/always on Halloween—and then we don't do it anymore.

Not after that Halloween.

And I'm gone and we smoke our family fires thicker with family secrets. Lies.

(Why didn't it all burn down?)

Oozing muck. Between adult toes. (And I am looking up. And there is no pit, there is no fire, and there is no steam. There are no clams.) I am looking up from the tree trunk drift log, sapwood sun-bleached white and wind/sand-fuzzed. Peering out. Beyond the curved point of our inlet river bay.

A single-mast skipjack. An oyster dredger.

That *Halloween.*

On its deck. A man in fisherman's sweater. Too far to discern. To recognize or to not. Watching me watching him.

Don't look. Not him. This time: Lynn, turn away.

Time tumbles. Back a single hour. Silas's Cadillac. Smells like his pipe—

Silas doesn't smoke anymore; he hasn't smoked for years. Look away!

DON'T DO THIS TO YOURSELF!

—and, having shaken ashes from the Dunhill bowl, he activates the window. Sealed closed. Close. The two of us. Sealed inside. Alone and closer than we've ever been or will ever be again.

"Dad, I don't get it. If it's so awful—"

"Unimaginably horrible."

*"—why does she suffer the pain? She won't take any-*thing?*"*

"After the chemo didn't work. Right at the beginning of this awful end, your mother took all of it. All at once."

"Mom tried to kill herself?"

"I was only just in time. After that...?" He puts his pipe to his mouth before remembering he's dumped it. *"They switched her to administered injection. She refused to let the nurse touch her. Any nurse. Any doctor. They stopped trying. She abused them. They stopped coming. Me: she won't let help. Says the pain will kill her faster. She begs to die."*

Oh, God—

Silas turns away; faces the manor house.

He's sobbing? Him?!

Won't let me see his tears.

"God damn it! Why didn't you call me before this? If I knew it had gotten this bad, I could've convinced her—"

"Michael and Hal are in the field." Distant. Not hearing. *"Gwen—seriously? And Melody, I could never ask..."*

"I said, 'Me.' You dismissive jerk."

Hard eyes over tear tracks. "You've come now." Holds up a white paper take-away sack. "And lookee here. Got us our clam chowder-Hallo'een-clambake."

Ignored. "I'm always around. I'm close. My office, my condo. Your stupid yellow phone works both ways. I'd've recognized the number. The urgency, I'd have dropped everything."

He stares at my face. "I didn't call you, girl, because you're drunk."

This time, I won't cry. I just won't.

Tears pool. "You're an asshole. Fuck you, Silas."

"Fuck me, fine, you're right. I am. But you've never been able to stop with one drink. Since that first sip—"

"I'm not a drunk. I'm an alcoholic."

"Ah, fuck you. You're not even that. An alcoholic can't stop. I know you can. And you're not a proper drunk; don't stumble around, lose control; you get by. You per-form. What you are *is a coward. Seen nothing like it. You drink to drown your courage because you're afraid of your own bravery. What you'd do with it."*

Me. Brittle. "What. Would. I. Ever *do with it?"*

He says, "Everything I can't. I've always been a cow-ard. At least I face that."

Means it. Meant it. It's always been this. I'm not even curious why. I'm cold. I'm stone.

"Don't. I'd rather hate you than pity you."

"She's asked me a thousand times."

Unsaid, I know what she's asked. To do what needs to be done. I know what he's asking me.

Don't live this again.

"We don't let dogs suffer the way we force it upon peo-ple. Hold each other to the strictest of unnatural laws..."

"I can't. Don't ask this of me."

"Well, she needs one of us. Tonight. And I've already betrayed her and failed."

That look. Again. Silas Kingston. My father. The cow-ard. "No one else in this family has the strength you have, daughter. Doris—almost; she tried—the mother who gave you *life. Bequeathed* you *that towering inner strength you hide from with booze. That woman who now can't end her own living hell. The two of you. The two of you share what we Kingston men can only admire and awe to. You are the real Kingston strength if you'd just lift your face out of that eighty-proof puddle."*

Why did you save your first/only/measly compliment for this?

Why did you recruit me to murder?

I draw air deeply. Through my mouth and into my lungs.

How did he get me here? So easily I hear my voice—my original voice, from child to woman, now cut from my throat.

Softly.

Holy.

Don't say it. I love you, Mom. I do, I do, I do—

I say it. "No one knows I'm here. You only bought one large soup, right? They'll only remember you, dinner for one. Just go out somewhere. I'll be gone when you come back. I'm going to need some time. Two hours?"

Silas nods, operational. "Two hours?"

"Yeah." Shame. "Need one to sober up."

He doesn't judge me. Just squeezes my knee, like he hasn't done since I was a girl.

Down the rickety stairs to the beach to collect myself. Finally, Daddy's "good girl."

My toes, unpolished, curl in sand and seashell muck.

A fisherman's sweater; the intricacies of the cable-knit pattern as he comes to me. Across the water in a launch.

Her balloon man.

Outboard putters. Putters onto the beach.

Her secret kisses. Clutches. Don't look.

I do not move. I bury my eyes. I see my toes. Remembered pink-polish-chipped.

Can I have a sip?

(I want it so fucking bad.)

He sits beside me. And I do not make a sound. Do not look. Imagine myself turned into a fish; I swim away from the devourous pike.

"You are Lynn."

Do not speak.

"I'd recognize you anywhere."

Her kaleidoscope man.

♕ ♕ ♕

My mother moans. Her eyelids draw apart. Red. Glowing. Pain. Alarm at the sight of me in the chair, quivering beside the door, smother pillow on my lap. Smother pillow gripped by both my hands, knuckles white, and on it, a moist imprint of my stricken face.

Hotel pillow wet against my face. It's Halloween. Wake up, Lynn.

That *Halloween, and I have never seen Doris defeated as I see her now. As she sees me.*

"Noooo. Linny." The tragedy of it all— "No. Not you, Linny"— of her life.

"Who is he?" I ask, and her pupils change. She knows everything—more than I—about who I've met. What he's said. What I know.

Her other man.

Red bleary eyes dart between mine and— "You're braver than this"— the smother pillow. "Sitting there. Sitting and mewling. Do what your father's afraid to. Love me. Finish me."

"If there's a chance— He says— The man says—"

"That man is a liar. There is no chance. There is nothing from that man except lies and destruction."

"I know liars. My world is liars. He wasn't lying."

"Everything that man says is a lie. Everything he's ever touched and placed and said, 'Beautiful/perfect,' he's set to be destroyed by his lies."

"He says he loves you." Hardest words ever: "I believe him. He says there's treatment. I believe that too. He wants me to bring you to his boat."

Doris seals her lips. All her strength it takes to hold them shut. To keep true words, untrusted, inside. Eyes dart wild; her mind scrambles.

I throw the pillow. I lunge. Slam my knees to the floor beside her. Where miracles happen. Grip her frail hands. She exhales. Red eyes roll back. She wilts.

Dead?

"Mom?"

Shallow pants. A swallow. "I don't care what he says. It would kill your father. My whole life would be only worth the value of its original sin. The lie that created me and all of us."

"You kissed him. I remember it, Mom. Why did you even take me? Make me see that?"

Wilts further but relaxes—no, surrenders to her words. "It was a bad idea. But understand: It wasn't wrong. He forced your father. He wanted to see Michael. Wanted to meet you. He had a right."

"It was more than once. You brought me a bunch of times. Times I don't remember Dad or Michael even being there. Like the time he gave me the kaleidoscope. The one Michael threw in the river when we got home."

The crack of a single chuckle from inside her throat. "It's not the book, but it's like the book, isn't it?"

"What book? That book?"

A strange peace. The wilting deepens. Her eyes un-moving behind translucent lids blue. A dream within a dream; her voice a dreamy edge. "Jenny's sins against her husband are complete. She accepts her death sentence. But Arthur won't. Arthur must not free her or his Round Table—justice for the sake of right, for the sake of justice—will be destroyed. As much as Arthur prays it, as it always happens throughout time—" Her eyes open— "Lance must not rescue Guenever. Please not this time."

"That's a damn storybook, Mom."

"It would make a mockery of Kaleidoscope. My kaleidoscope." *She looks at me. The pain is gone. She savors her sorrow.* "It would kill the only two men I love."

"What are you talking about? You love him?! All these years—some kind of affair—forever?"

"I was faithful to your father. Always. And he knew everything."

Headlights from below wash the window. Wash the wall. Paint the ceiling.

"Is that Silas?"

I nod. Feel my bottom lip, fat. I might as well be four years old waiting for the mermaid to rise from the fountain with the sword.

"If they're both here— You cannot let either man inside. Go. Lock everything. Stop them."

I do.

Doris hangs in fire.

⚜ ⚜ ⚜

LYNN SHUDDERED. "Fire!" Lunged forward in the hotel bed. Arms flailed. Limbs twisted in sheet tangle. Thrashed and crashed, tumbled onto the floor. "Fire...?"

Lynn's eyes: level with the tipped over, half-empty bottle of gin. Wrapped its neck in her tingling fist.

"Fire. All fire. And ash. For shit."

The turret room. Her vision tracked to the recessed counter. The glass of gin Roman poured her last night. The glass she never touched. Lynn shoved to her feet.

Fire engulfs Doris. Engulfs— Love letters? Diaries? Secrets. Russian.

Lynn bolted the gin. Gin thick and hot down her new throat.

Fire.

Fleeing. Let the whole place burn.

Foxtail Farm refused. History refused. Silas refused.

Her stomach lurched. Lynn lurched. The bathroom. Vision lurched. The toilet. A blast of vomit. The sink. Twisted cold-water tap. In the mirror, Lynn recognized the bottle in her fist. In the mirror, Lynn recognized *that* Lynn, who leered back, saying "yes."

Lynn wrenched the cork. Drank the half remaining; one go of it. Released the bottle, gripped the counter—done this before—shoved her face beneath the running spigot. Gulped water until the alcohol stayed down.

Flames blossomed inside her. Red, yellow, orange licks dancing between, hot—

I'll have to file a report. Explain fucking this guy, this target entity—

I'm so fucked—

Saw stars. Didn't fight her consciousness. Didn't fight her conscience.

I got him, though. Michael, I'm going over the wall. See you/find you. Azerbaijan.

Lynn fell back. Hit the floor. Black marble chilled the length of her naked body. Her mouth slackened—and maybe she'd always wanted to fall back—patterned goofy, a clownish grin. The brightest, saddest smile of them all.

2.

"THE WALGREENS AND CVS'ES are what put me out of business here in Leonardtown. But before them, when your father-in-law, Silas Kingston, could've been going down to the chain drugstores in Lexington Park—I knew him by wave-hellos on the street. In that big old car of his—and he'd come in. And I'd 'How's she doing—?' Doris, his poor wife; so awful. 'Specially with the advances made fighting that exact cancer that took her. You know, counter chit-chat we'd have."

Head throb/wound throb. Melody washed down a Vicodin with beer.

"Silent, Silas Kingston. I remember him. Very serious." Raised index finger to replace an unspoken "But"— "Witty, when he *would* speak. If you take your humor on the dry side." Here, Walt Samuels gave Melody a wry and questioning look.

"I do—I can—I mean, I see that in him."

Whir.

Halloween night. Melody sat with Victoria—from the Historical Society—and her father inside the Samuels's sunroom. Walt drank Kentucky bourbon; the women had beer. Jack and Little Silas manned the trick-or-treat door with Mrs. Samuels.

"Feel free, boys, to call me Ellen but put a 'witch' at the front. Witch Ellen—" still wearing her pointy alewives' hat— "Let's scare some kids opening the door fast on 'em, before the ding-dong, huh?"

"Was his father," Walt went on, "Harold Kingston. I knew him better, and I'll tell you why."

Why did Hal move his gun to his hip?

"Old Man Kingston, and who am I to talk? Sixty-seven this year, but back when I was fresh out of pharmacist college, and all the chain stores were coming into Lexington Park servicing the Naval Air Station. Pulling in all the county shoppers with cheap goods. One-stop, low prices crap—pardon me—"

Who in Old Town would be a threat to Hal? To me and the twins?

"Old Man Kingston, that'd be Harry—what they called him—and his wife, I don't recall her name." Probed Melody with bourbon bright eyes.

Vicodin and beer: from *whir* to *jjjhhhirrr* as the pill dissolved. Eased into Melody's brain. Eased her pain, and then some. A smile wiggled her lips. "Uh. You know, I'm not sure I remember her name." Melody checked her phone.

Victoria jumped in. "I remember. It's Amelia. She was instrumental in the Kingston collection we have, and Melody, I want to talk to you about what I found. About your family—"

"Vicky, don't interrupt your father. This is a good story. About a good deed. Good people—Harry and Abigail."

"Amelia." Victoria.

"That's right." Sipped bourbon. "My mistake. My father told me—and that man never lied—those Kingstons set up, with the old First Farmer Bank, a grant for small businesses. Money to go toward competitive pricing and local marketing. They must have planned it a long time, because in sixty-eight, when I stepped onto the filling platform beside my dad, all the family businesses had already registered. Right around the holidays, received a check and some rules for the year and a paperwork agreement only an idiot wouldn't sign to keep it rolling over. Even Bob Anderson, with the used car lot—slippery as they come—and this won't come as a surprise to you, Mrs. Kingston, but 'specially slippery toward our black brethren."

Victoria huffed. Melody gave her a wan look. Walt Samuels breezed on.

"That was back then. Now we're integrated and all that..."

"Dad. Please."

"All I'm saying is that civic generosity went on even after Harry and Abigail pulled up stakes and vanished to Paraguay or Portugal or wherever it was after Silas moved home with his bride." Zeroed back on Melody. "You married yourself into some fine stock, little lady. Founding stock. Real patriots to these parts and good on'ya, movin' up."

Walt wanted to clink his highball glass with Melody's beer bottle. Melody buried her face in her phone, tapping it to no purpose.

Jjjhhhirrr.

Victoria misinterpreted. "Refill, Dad?" On purpose. "Let me." Snatched his glass. Under her breath— "As if you need more—" Went to the cocktail cart.

Come on, Hal. Check in. Couple a'racists—old guy, with her trying to make nice.

"These white gloves we'd like you to wear while handling the documents."

Victoria thrust the glass into her father's hand and before Melody knew what was happening, gripped Melody's hand—who yelped. Pulled her out of her chair. Led Melody through the glass-paned storm door. Outside to the deck.

"It's the home I grew up in. Embarrassing."

Melody knew she shouldn't. Hit the beer. "We all got fathers."

She wants to be friends. Probably as short in that department as I am. And when did I ever let race get under my skin? Never noticed it before, now it's all I'm thinking about. Boone-fucking-Kelso.

I killed Mama. Not Boone.

"Dad means well, but his size ten shoe fits too easily into his size twelve mouth."

"Words/ways of saying things—not something I get upset over. I'm not upset. I like your father."

"He's *generally* likeable." They clinked beer bottles. No harm. No foul. Both took obligatory sips. "Whatever your husband went after, if it was something bad—and I hope not—I've, well, I hate to think what he's done to them." Dramatic saucer eyes dashed with mischief.

When Victoria followed her comment about Hal with a remark that her own behavior at the Colonel Vickery House might have come off worse than Walt's,

Melody laughed and explained about the moth. How, the moment they met, all she was thinking was that winged vampire bat-beast burrowing into her hair. They laughed some more.

Beer sips. Vicodin tremolo.

A finger waved at Melody's stitches, her partially shaved head. "Guess it came back for you?"

"Was an owl. A whole bunch."

"Whoa. Halloween, no less. Sort of makes you look like—"

"Sally from Nightmare Before Christmas?"

Big grin. "Kinda-sorta does."

We could be friends.

Melody gave a hopeful smile, but Victoria's face went somber and intent. She tiptoed her words carefully. "I like to approach history like a good mystery. Look at that. I rhymed. I enjoy digging around. Discovering the secret-secrets."

"The Kingston secrets, I'd say, are the most awful I've ever read."

The sole of Mama's foot is the color of the top of my foot. Except for the blood.

Want a murder mystery? Look no further than Ragdoll.

"I tried to warn you, Melody. And I am sorry. But when I was cleaning up, there was this kind of a clue. It always bothered me, but I couldn't identify what it was. Then my eye—like things happen—just fell on it."

"I'll tell you what it was. That Turkey John Swan was a serial killer. And all the Silas Kingstons were his willing accomplices, and that instinct is in my own children's blood—I mean, if that sort of thing carries in the blood."

Her phone vibrated.

Thank God, Hal. How. I. Love. You.

"That's my—"

Victoria touched her arm to stay her thoughts. "I don't know about genetics, but I don't think it works that way. With that sort of thing. What I do know is I found some stuff—"

Melody read the incoming text. "Hal says we should call a car to take us home. What's your address here?"

Victoria walked them to the street. The twins, having eaten all the leftover Fun Size bars from Witch Ellen's bowl, sugar-jacked and making it known this was the best Halloween ever, Victoria pressed her point as the car arrived.

"There's no record of Turkey John Swan ever accepting a reward."

Loading the kids. "He took scalps. Right? Serial killers and personal souvenirs?"

"That's just it. There was a court case where he couldn't produce the body."

"Victoria: thank you for tonight. But you need to drop this."

"The scalp he produced in court was sheep's wool. Counterfeit."

Jjjhhheeerr... Pain killers with half a beer. Dizzy. Dumb, dumb, dumb.

Victoria saw. Steadied Melody with a gentle hand. "Please, Melody, I want to dig at this, but I won't get much leeway with the Society's director if I don't have you requesting my help. If I don't have you digging with me."

Like why would I ever do that?

The wind kicked up. The trees shook. The leaves, flapping, made the sound of chattering teeth. Melody found herself clutching Victoria's hands.

Whiiirrr, jjjhhheerrr, whiiirrr. Gotta get home. Head. Not. Right.

"I don't know." She released her friend.

Friend. Mmm.

Tilted into the car. Pressed both hands to her heart. "I don't think I could handle it."

"Something's very wrong with that whole story. Please?"

Closing the door: "Okay. Whatever. I'll call you."

♛ ♛ ♛

A STOP IN OLD TOWN to scoop up Charlotte and Leigh who, wide-eyed, said, "We've never stayed out for the whole party;" Charlotte, made sure Melody didn't think *they thought* she forgot them. "That was the most awesomest Halloween ever. Where's Uncle Hal? Where's your truck?"

"He got called in."

And the girls nodded and went about comparing notes for the fourth and fifth time; all that made their late night out their most awesome Halloween of all.

Melody tucked her rowdy twins into bed. She checked in on the girls. Leigh already asleep. Charlotte finishing an Instagram collage, then phone off and a "Goodnight/Happy Halloween" exchange from the door and Melody headed downstairs. A sidelong glance at Doris looming on the landing wall. Emanated a peculiar sorrow Melody hadn't noticed before. A whiff of smoke made Melody stop. Sniffed, but it was gone; might not have been at all. Gazed up at the haunted/haunting altogether teasing cerulean blue of Doris's eyes. On second glance—a trick of moonlight—no, she hadn't noticed anything.

I wish I knew how you lasted so long. If you hadn't had gotten sick, you'd be here to help me through.

A laugh to herself.

I don't even know you and I miss you.

I miss my *mother.*

Doris's feet. Her ballroom shoes. Red glitter, gold lace accents. The light and shadow accent made the closed toes shine like blood.

Melody felt the weight of the pistol, the pistol she killed her mother with, clutched in her hand. She opened her fingers. All she held was the pharmacy vial.

Melody hurried to the kitchen. She filled a tall glass with water. Opened her pills.

"Don't think you should do that." Silas interrupted her from the doorway as she was about to pour them down the sink.

"They dull more than the pain." She turned the bottle upright. Placed it, full, on the counter and faced him. "I almost forgot and left the girls behind at the green."

Silas capped the vial. "Better to have them if you need them, than wish in pain you hadn't flushed them."

Melody watched his eyes. He watched hers. She drank deeply from her water glass.

"No Hal back with you?"

"He got pulled away."

Silas nodded, like checking off an action item. "Wouldn't worry."

"Never do. Never ask."

He gestured to the porch. A soft, inviting sofa. She adjusted pillows so her wounded back matched a gap between them. Put up her feet. He settled into his wing-back reading chair.

"I am in a sorry state, Papa."

"Even as sorry as you feel—"

"—and look."

"Look at you: You are admirable, Melody Kingston. The most perspicacious of all my children."

Overcome by anticipation and dread. "I'm not one, really."

"One of my children? You think?"

A shrug. A wince at the tug of stitches. "And I don't even know what that other word means."

A glint of amusement. "You will when I say this..."

He didn't speak. She craned her neck. A pointed look. He said, "Now you do."

Melody narrowed her eyes. Pondered. "I know things without them having to be said?"

"You bet, you do. You see around the edges, the be-hind of things; a ready insight without needing explana-tion. You get the nature of the what's-what others never notice. Keenly so."

A stirring inside that wasn't the pills. "That's kind—you saying that. I try. But I wasn't very per-sp-whatever as far as those owls went. If you hadn't come along..."

"Maybe the owls weren't the thing you've been trying to discern on your solitary hikes in our little wilderness."

He knows.

Does he know?

Is he talking about himself with his perspica-cious-ness?

"You know where Hal is, don't you?"

"Not where. Not necessary. But I know with whom. He'll be home. He'll have a challenge and a choice and—I predict—whatever he chooses, getting there is going to make him difficult to live with until he decides. But I know you just as well. And this agitation you're feeling—not the owls, not the pills, not Hal—it's be-cause, that you're always available to everyone else, you never avail yourself to you. And right now, because you need to be focused entirely on yourself, you're struggling with a kind of—I don't know—feeling of selfishness?"

Melody nodded, wary.

"Because, my sunny girl, you carry something."

Melody bunched shoulders, drawing all her tension inward. Cowered from him. Silas lifted his hand.

"Wait. No need to be defensive. It's private. It's a secret. I know that. And I would never ask you to divulge. Ever."

She collapsed backwards. Gave a little cry of pain as her back rubbed the pillows wrong. Deflated. "You don't know the half of it."

"Now's not the time to tell me even a quarter."

Melody drifted her gaze. The bookcase and the shelves. The bar. The television dark. Anywhere but Silas and her desire to unburden. Tell it all.

"Now's the time for you to listen to me. Look at me, Melody."

Don't look. Don't do it.

She forced her gaze to wander. The windows. The night. So black, so bleak. A reflection in the glass of Doris's book on its stand. He went on anyway.

"If I know about one thing—and more than half of what people think I know only exists in their assumption—the one thing I *do* know, unequivocally about, perfectly, and with full knowledge, is secrets. Making them. Keeping them. Forcing them and stealing them." She didn't quite know when she focused, only that Silas was smiling at her. "Buying them, trading them, fabricating, passing, treasuring, bleeding for and breaking and blowing them up."

She felt his love.

"Phew. Hi," he said.

With an effort she returned her heart to him. "Do me a favor, Papa, and don't go telling me any of yours. I don't have room."

"My secrets are safe with me."

He lifted the chair by its arms. Scooted closer.

"I'm going to ask you some questions."

Right up to her. He laid his hands flat, palms up in his lap. Supplication? Surrender? Whatever it was, it put her further at ease.

"Don't reveal anything," he said. "Just a little survey to help you understand—not the secret itself—but how secrets make us feel. Remember, it's my one skill. You ready?"

He moved his knee between her two knees; she noticed this, the tinge of togetherness/trust it gave her. Melody nodded.

"Say it, Melody."

"I'm good. Go on." Then, "I'm ready, yes. Ask away."

"Okay. Can you live with yourself without revealing it?"

"I always have."

"And it hasn't affected you?"

Melody shook her head. Remembered his instruction, "No." She felt strange. Like the inside Melody was stepping away from her. She heard herself saying, "It's becoming like a hole, and the edges keep collapsing, and it gets bigger, and suddenly things that were safe, things that weren't near the edge, are about to tip over it. Into the hole. It's starting to."

"Affect you."

"Affect me. And I'm afraid it's all going to collapse in on itself and bury me. Bury everyone."

"That collapsing—" He wagged his fingers, open in his lap; Melody felt further apart from herself as she watched her hands rest on top of his. "Sometimes, that collapsing ends up filling the hole. Like magic—because you didn't expect it—it lifts you and everyone out."

"No. Not this, it won't. It's going to bury me." Pained eyes. "It will. I know it."

Silas bobbed his head, unconcerned. Rubbed his white thumbs on the tobacco brown backs of her hands. "You don't have to answer any question I'm going to ask you that makes you uncomfortable. Okay?"

"Okay."

"Good. How long have you had this secret?"

"Since I was a little girl. Very little." Another strange wave washed over her. Like the two Melody's had suddenly rejoined as one and she stared at him wondering if he felt it in her hands. He showed no reaction, but his face was as sensitive as she had ever seen it.

Flash! His secret is his nobility.

"Don't drift. Meet my eyes. Is this the first time you feel it challenged?"

"No. I guess it's been challenged, I don't know, constantly, more and more as life gets bigger. More complicated. No. That's not right. More important—life. To me. Does that make sense?"

"The stakes get higher the more you have to lose?"

"Yes."

"What you have to lose? What's most precious of all? When everything else is cut away, I assume, is your family. Hal, and Jack and Little Silas. The fundamental unit: mother/father/children. You're willing to give your life—and I mean that in real living-versus-dead terms—for their safety? Their peace? Their honor and their happiness?"

And with this ring, I am Kingston.

Her eyes burned; Melody didn't cry. Never cried. Nodded, yes.

"Say it. It'll feel better."

"Yes. One hundred percent, yes."

"Good. And you haven't acted in any way against those truths?"

"Never."

"This secret would never lead you to do anything dishonest to intentionally hurt them?"

"No, I'd never—" It struck her. Fast. Hard. Electric. Lightning. When she spoke, it was as much in answer to Silas as to herself. Unnerved and, in that, awed. "It's my own honesty I'm afraid of."

Her anxiety left her. Because no opposing/conquering emotion swept in to replace it, all she could do was surrender to herself.

Silas watched Melody's transfiguration. He brought their hands together, hers lightly clasped in his. Lifted in the air between them.

"Whatever winter brings us—and have no illusion, this may be our most brutal winter—you'll be alright with this. And, more importantly, you will see Hal and my lambs safely through the storm."

"A storm is coming?"

Why do I know he means more than the weather?

He held her hands as he rose, releasing them as he shifted, delicately, out of her personal space. For one moment, Melody's hands, flat together, long, slender fingers extended, hovered upright before her eyes.

"I think we both should go to our beds and sleep as long as we possibly can. Deep and as dreamless as we can hope for. You okay?"

She rubbed her thighs with open palms. Nodded. Met her father-in-law's gaze, peacefully, once more. "You already know. My secret. Don't you?"

Silas dismissed it with a laugh. "I know that I love: My. Very perspicacious. Daughter. Sleep tight, Melody."

The screen door slow-creaked its closing soundtrack as he disappeared into the darkness.

Melody shut the light. Melody went upstairs. She crawled into bed where her subconscious ignored Silas Kingston's instructions.

She dreams of Turkey John Swan. Fearsome with bloody tomahawk, swift feet bear down upon her. Through an ancient cellar door. Down musty stairs.

Terrorized, Melody hides among the wine racks of the North Vista Outhouse. The scalphunter stalks her, aisle by aisle, calling, "Here little doggy," purring and hissing and clacking his tomahawk blade against bottles in echoes of the owls.

A high, harsh whisper from behind. "Melody. This way."

Dredged from memories of the Fourth of July, Melody stands before the secret panel. Open. The figure of a buckskin girl dark in the low door's shadow. Melody ducks. Peers inside. She stares at herself. The way she remembers her face, her hair, her round and frightened eyes the night she shot her mother.

But it isn't her. The hairs on her neck rise from Turkey John Swan's hot breath behind her.

"Good, child. Nika, meet your twin. This is Melody."

Nika says, "I'm her. She's me."

Melody shakes as though her body will fall apart. Otherwise, she cannot move. And although her lips are sealed, her voice rings clear. "The Lord giveth."

Nika takes Melody's hand. "The water show us forth."

Nika pulls.

"Go in. Go in. It isn't a mystery. Go in, woman."

Melody resists. Fights. To go inside is to die. Nika vanishes. Melody whirls.

Turkey John Swan: vanished.

The secret panel? Shut and hidden in the wall.

Awake. Alone. Shivering fear. Melody noticed the clockface. Stared. Recalled her earlier nightmare. Since Paige's birthday.

A serpent's tongue uncoils and wags inside Boone Kelso's open mouth. Words roar from his throat: "Coming, child. Coming soon for you. Soon for them. Better find my be-all/end-all-American-dream-damnation."

Each night she awoke from it to face the clock. 4:12 or 4:13 or 4:15. Never 4:14.

Until now.

3.

"Ever worry your fat is going to kill you?"

"My grandmother was four inches shorter and at least fifty pounds heavier. She lived to ninety-five. Do have the sandwich, Hal."

"You're what, three hundred pounds?"

"The sandwich."

"I don't want your sandwich."

"But it is your sandwich. I have my sandwich right here." Drexler pulled a foot-long sub, oozing an orange substance—close to, maybe mixed-with mayonnaise—from its wrapper. Pulled from a Quiznos bag he'd brought inside with him and down the stairs. Quiznos bag on the floor beside his open briefcase. The sandwich Hal didn't want in the middle of a water-ringed/veneer-warped uncared for red oak dining table meant for another house. In another room. A room that wouldn't have a concrete floor. This room, this basement illuminated by a chain-hung fluorescent shop light, did.

Quiznos wrappers, wadded napkins lay near and around a red Rubbermaid wastebasket. Too close to the water heater. White and rusty and gas-fired. Cycling/flaring. An on-purpose hint at the chance of an accident going terribly wrong. And the chairs, five of them—Morton Drexler and Hal Kingston, the basement's only occupants, occupying two—though each came in a shade of red, came from three unmatched sets. The sort of set-up trained inquisitors set up to stress a psychological mood of random danger. Cast-off displacement. Never forget impermanence.

"There's a microwave upstairs. Would you prefer a little heat on it? One of my assis—"

"I don't want your fucking sandwich."

"Trick or treat yourself." Scoffed. Indignant. Eyebrows-raised, skeptical, the kind of expression that wrinkles brows, though Drexler's—too thick, soft, too pliable—didn't wrinkle. His forehead just rippled and flowed. Expansive. "You're angry. I get it." Conciliatory, sniffled, underwhelmed.

Associate Deputy Director, Counterintelligence, Morton Drexler unwrapped his sandwich. Gooey lettuce fringed its meaty edges. Free of the wrapper, orangey mayo-y sauce plopped. All over. Drexler paid attention to achieving a just right, a good, double-fisted grip. Lifted a heel end to moist lips and said (not caring it was while biting/chewing), "Still thinking about shooting me, I reckon. Wishing you hadn't let me lift your iron. Eh?"

"I recall I handed it over in the spirit of my cooperation with your credential."

Hal disliked Drexler with the instinctivity dogs suffer for cats. Like a dog with a cat, it knows it is heavier, bigger, it's stronger—jaws more powerful—but it fears cats for their individualistic disdain. Their antisocial, solitary nature. The dog learns that in any fight with a cat, just like with a car, it will get all tangled up, batted into the air, tossed on its ass and lose. The dog's heart, ever faithful to a naïve and sentimental nobility always rushes into folly; the cat knows what a dog is. What it will do once away from the pack. What to do with it.

As far as eating habits, sandwiches in particular, most cats were tidier than Morton Drexler.

Revolted, Hal continued. "Fun fact. Did you know they have Quiznos in Cairo?"

"Ain't something I noticed for never having been—" Chewed. "There." Grinned.

"Well, in Cairo, bread's crustier. Harder, you know. I met up with a Daesh recruiter in Cairo. Once. Table out front of that Quiznos. View of Saint Mary's Maadi Church. View of the Nile. Not as obese as you—"

"Obesity is a disease. If you're going to remark on the thirty-three percent of my mass that is less of me than the sixty-seven percent that isn't, I'm happy with your earlier pejorative 'fat.'"

"A *fat* ISIS recruiter eating a Quiznos. Just like yours. The Cairo Quiznos was one of his stops. Twice, sometimes three times a week, where he'd troll for hungry, lost, needy boys. Start by buying them a meal."

Gnawing. Cautious. A one-*ha* laugh—the kind meant to say fake laugh/fake funny/not funny at all. "This is bound to get unpleasant."

Beneath the atrocious white summer-linen suit, sweat-stained yellow, vaguely villainous and purposely so, Drexler's was an obesity unwrinkled and soft. Altogether rounded and kind of glorious and pleasing in its own right, like time-worn Texas hills thick and downy. Raw and unpleasant in winter.

And winter was coming.

"Then you know how these Daesh pukes do it. Promise them three squares. Promise them Syrian pussy. Take 'em to camp. Teach 'em the fight songs. Rape their asses, then jack 'em up on heroin, meth, Ritalin—whatever it takes to strap a kid into a suicide belt and send 'em running and shrieking Allah's great goodness to kingdom come."

"And the bacon—?" His eyes had crow's-feet at their corners which, squeezing, he could make himself appear humorous or ironic, or possessed of unwavering discernment. Chomped again. Chewed again. "—Without all the sizzle?"

"Heel of my hand, heel of the bread. One good pop." Before Drexler could react, Hal demonstrated: stopping half-an-inch short of the gooey sandwich and the fat man's life. "I killed him."

Anyone else would have hit the floor. That size, anyone else would have hit it hard, but this ponderous man—a fascinating thing about Morton Drexler, and it was to Hal, observing him—was that deep within his girth was a man of ginger steps and nimble balance and, if not gainly in reflex, smooth in reaction. Morton Drexler did a tip-toey kind of pirouettish turn around the back of his chair. Fred Astaire with the hat rack. Resumed his seat from the other side.

Hal gaped. Drexler lamented his sandwich, tossed in the scuffle, while at the top of the stairs, the door flew wide. The pair of officers Hal manhandled on the sidewalk near Victoria Samuel's house barged inside.

Drexler flung a hand at the air. They halted.

To Hal. "Shame. That was a Queso Philly Steak. Very delicious." He dipped chins at the one he offered Hal. "Was going to get to this at some point."

What—? The scuffle? The sandwich? Fifty/fifty.

To his officers. "Y'all might as well scoot on home—the good you'll never do me here."

The pair hesitated, uncertain.

"Mr. Kingston has shown that if he wanted to harm me, I'd already be dead." Another dismissive wave. "And leave his weapon in the drawer of the hall table, would-ja?"

They shuffled out. Drexler reached down. Shuffled papers onto the tabletop. "You've established—more times than I should have let you—what you're adept at. Well, here's how I earn my keep. So, wash off your warpaint and listen."

Three files. Logo'd/color-striped/branded *Classified, Secret,* and the last, *Top Secret.*

Pink hydrangea hand on the first. "This one's about you. I imagine you wish it was 'Secret,' or higher, but it ain't. Too obvious what it tells. And what it tells me is Hal Kingston's gone dug up more snakes than he can kill."

Documents dealt like cards.

"Official transcript of your debriefing, jetting back from your little Turkey trot. Sworn and signed that your brother, our officer, Mr. Michael Kingston—although unable to be rescued—escaped with his life after your fire team's encounter with the late Colonel Vural of the Turkish National Intelligence Organization. Look-see?"

Hal said nothing. Did nothing.

"Recognize this here document beside it?"

Nothing.

"Want to tell me what it is?"

Hal took air. In through his nose. Measured out between lips. An illusion of relaxation.

"Your follow-up statement. Sworn. La-dee-da signed."

Nodded Hal to offer something. Hal did not.

"In it, you recant your original debriefing statement. Swear to the fact that, to the best of your knowledge, better clarity upon recollection, and all that, you witnessed your brother KIA'd in Turkey. That you have no doubt he was killed in action and is deceased."

Drexler masked his face with sympathy. A few sympathetic nods that trailed off cheeks like a pair of pink balls running out of bounce. "Go from MIA to KIA. There's a fellow been carving stars in our Memorial Wall for twenty-five years. Just about ready to chisel the one you verify for Michael. No one'll take kindly if that turns out a lie. Holes like that, in marble, don't patch."

"Are you accusing me of some kind of criminal act?"

Fucking Michael. Fucking Dad. Fucking Gwen.

Outwardly cold. Outwardly marble.

"It's the thing gets me dancing in the hog trough, though. I'll tell you. Not the violating of your oath. Not the defrauding of the US Government with death benefit payouts to your pa."

"Called it like I saw it. Turkey's an ally. There's an investigation. Been no payouts. No one's getting ready to carve a damn thing."

Drexler grabbed the Hal sandwich. Tore the paper. Tore a bite. Big bite. Spoke through tearing teeth. "Hate to see you dig that snake pit much deeper, but Hal—" Big swallow. Ran his tongue over his top teeth, and full circle. Tops and bottoms. Pointed to the third report. "You flew to Milan the day after you filed that second, corrective statement."

"Visited a friend. He'll vouch for me."

"I know. Major Pietro Vianello. Retired from the Italian Lagunari Regiment. Is he the one who provided the weapon?"

Vegas quick, the three doc sets swept back into their *Classified* cover. Drexler dealt his next cards from the *Secret* file.

Photos: Switzerland. Helene Favre's street. Hal entering the bar/café where he uploaded the SIM card. Seespiegal restaurant; interior. Print from a kitchen security video. Hal random-captured, corner of the bar. Seespiegal; exterior. Crime scene photo. Dead guy out back. Last photo: The Coop market coffee bar. Michael. Full face, paying for coffees. Thrilling smile.

Next. "Air Italia manifests." First: "Dulles-Milan. Got your buddy Vianello's car crossing into—" nod to the pics— "Switzerland." Second manifest: "Milan-Dulles. Sorry your brother didn't opt to come home with you the *second* time you offered the favor, Captain Kingston. You don't need me to make you understand, your corrective statement hand-in-hand with your subsequent travel: I can burn you hotter than a pot of neck bones."

Just doesn't quit with that folksy shit.

Drexler collected photos back to the *Secret* folder. Back inside it except for the shot of the shot-dead guy. "You did that." Met Hal's gaze with wrinkle-edged eyes. "Hal. None of this goes away."

"What do you want me to do about it?"

Drexler bounced his rubber face a few more times, failing to catch a smile, then pushed aside the first two folders. Centered *Top Secret* in front of him. Opened the cover. Fresh photo prints facedown in a pile.

"I come from a card playing part of the country. Did you know that?"

"I know I don't care."

"Folks do. Folks appreciate it. So much so, they named the most popular variant of poker after us."

He dealt the top two photographs face down to Hal.

"You gotta be fucking kidding me."

"Play along. I put my all into stacking the deck."

Hal's turn to scoff. Crossed his arms.

"Come on. Pick 'em up, Hal. Ain't going to bite. Look."

"What do you think we're playing for?"

"What do you think? The old man who got you into this mess." He readied the next three photos. "Silas Kingston. Now, I said, 'Take. A. Look.'"

Hal turned them over. Two three-letter agency ID shots. Two men. Both 1980s versions of clean-cut. First one, recognizable to anyone in the CIA. Especially a Kingston.

Edward Lee Howard.

The second was unknown to Hal. Early thirties. Dark-haired. A mustache longer than matched the haircut. Were he to guess, Hal would guess it typical FBI, wig-ready-undercover agent.

"You know traitor Howard, seeing how your daddy flushed him. Curious about the other?"

"Deal."

Drexler turned the next three photos face up.

One: The FBI undercover man. Ten years earlier. Special Forces graduation. Mom and pop and a green beret.

Two: The FBI undercover man. Scene of the Howard fuck-up; dumbfounded beside a car, gawping at the be-wigged mannequin Howard's wife jack-in-the-boxed in the passenger seat to fool him when Howard hotfooted it to Mexico/Helsinki/Moscow.

What the fuck? Some former Green Beret/FBI under-cover jackass who followed the wife and lost Silas's catch to the Soviets. Thirty years ago.

Three: The no-longer FBI undercover man. More recent. Few years. Desert tan.

We all got tan. Fucking deserts.

Man in his prime. Become the type who assumes he's surveilled. Makes sure—always—he's wearing a fuck-you smirk on his mug; a just-try-an'-touch-me twinkle in his eye.

Real Major Dad dicksuck.

The graying tight/rakish mustache over-compensating for salt-and-pepper ring-around-the-bald spot. Wears the playing Army insignia-free OCIE military uniform and gear of war zone private outfit privateers. Off to the side of some oil executives/engineers. War damaged Iraqi oil fields. A group of Private Military Company operators back up *Major Dad*.

Hal chills. One of those PMC mercs: same guy he popped/dropped in Switzerland.

"Ready for the Turn?"

Hal dipped his chin. Drexler's fourth photo. Face up. Middle of the table. A kick in the balls. The three SWAT/not SWAT killers. Dulles International. Fourth a'July. Parking lot security video capture; pulling off balaclavas. Ready to haul ass. Not in a police vehicle, but a waiting, blacked-out "Bebe's Better Blooms" flower van. Same guy he killed—part of this group, too—while beside him: guy he saw kidnap Pinwheel. That's two. Number three? Never seen him in person, but recognizes him now. All three of them are part of the merc team backing *Major Dad* back in the Iraq photo.

Hal considered Drexler. In for a penny? Nods.

Drexler flipped the last photo. The River Card. "Would you look at that?"

A leafy street. A Starbucks. A thumb drive passed Silas to—

"Who the hell is this FBI dicksuck/Major Dad looking bitch?"

"Name's Finn Houton. Your father's a forgiving man. Houton fucks up the arrest of your daddy's prize, CIA traitor/Soviet spy Edward Lee Howard, back in '85. Houton's fuck-up lets Howard escape to Moscow. Yet here's your pa with Houton, back in March and breaking bread."

"Any idea what Silas passed him?"

"Absolutely. That's my job. See, Houton's private army contracts for us. Was going back to Iraq, his group to run security on a POW camp."

"Isn't he a little late? Almost a year since our last troops pulled out."

"You'd think. But this camp's special. Prisoners there don't necessarily want to go home."

"And that's why?"

"Iranian Sunnis. About one hundred and fifty of them. Spilled over the border in the Iraqi Civil War to fight Shia militants and the Islamic State in Iraq."

"These the Jundallah guys Secretary Clinton designated a terror group, few years back?"

"It's become a sticky question."

"What's my father's involvement?"

"Not supposed-to-be involved. Before he and Harker
sashayed back on the floor, that is. Now Silas done got
involved. Doing what? Well, the rest of the Agency is not
so sure."

"But you've got ideas."

"Let's just say, to *me*, this doesn't much look like a
prison camp anymore." Hydrangea hand into his folder.
"Let's call this a Wild Card."

Satellite imagery. POW camp. Modified. Cage fencing: gone. Gun towers: facing out. Instead of in. Gobs of
men. Uniformed. Organized. Armed.

Hal. Incredulous. "I've had the pleasure of hitting
those. Afghanistan. Libya. Yemen. Syria. That's a terror
training camp."

"Designated KALEIDOSCOPE. Turns out every time
Mr. Houton turns up—" Drexler riffled the *Top Secret*
folder— "Silas Kingston hops right on it. Whatever the
op, it gets KALEIDOSCOPE red-flagged. All the way
back to..."

He put the photograph of Edward Lee Howard on top
of all of them. "The one who got away."

Drexler swept up all the photos. Grabbed the three
folders. Game over, he jumbled them together. Shoved
them into his briefcase. Hal shook his head. To clear it.
Shake out the bad ideas. Worse thoughts worse.

"Drexler, you know as well as any Kingston: my father
is an asshole. A devious asshole. But above all else, the

man is a patriot. I don't know this Houton, and he's not my business. Howard escaped; that's on the FBI—"

"FBI fired Houton over it. Gave yo' daddy a black eye, yet Silas Kingston's been propping him up ever since." Half-garbled in transmission, Drexler working weird his mouth with his tongue.

"My father charged right back with the successful investigation and capture of Aldrich Ames."

"After almost a decade of Ames running free-agent against us."

Drexler's gaze probed. Behind his lips his tongue worked overtime. Hal shifted on his red chair. Leather creaked.

"What about Hanssen? That was as much Dad's as FBI."

Drexler's lips parted. A glimpse of tongue like a fat eel doing its thing around the fat man's teeth. "I was around for that one. Part of the Silas Kingston team." Finger in to wrangle the eel. "Daddy-o's biggest contribution was us looking at someone else. Hal, you say you're familiar with KALEIDOSCOPE?"

Hal fascinated Drexler's mouth with disgust. "Didn't say. And what the fuck you doing with your mouth?"

"Lettuce in these Quiznos. Shred it too small. Little pieces git between the teeth. Since you bring it up—" Drexler unbent a paperclip. Used it as a toothpick. Finished the job. "See? Lettuce."

Dropped the wire on the floor. Drummed his thumbs on the table's edge. Recentered focus on Hal. Walrus'd a sigh. "In my experience—because I was Silas's right hand for so long, while his left hand covered my eyes—it was my experience when KALEIDOSCOPE came into the equation, we'd see your father's hand."

"How many hands you figure he's got?"

"Man's a veritable octopus."

"You work Counterintelligence. Not me."

"Yes. The fat kid emptying the wastebasket who made it to the top. Until I started knocking on the KALEIDO-SCOPE door. Found myself out with the trash. Now, it may be KALEIDOSCOPE goes back to the times before World War One. There's indication it was in place long before the Agency opened its doors. But that might be old frosting on a new cake baked in the USSR when your father was sent there by the old counter-intel kingpin James Jesus Angleton—make the sign of the cross." But he didn't.

"My dad didn't work for Angleton then. Angleton investigated my father hard after Moscow."

"And I'm wondering if that wasn't fairy-dust all this time."

"You think my father's doubled? Been playing both sides all these years?"

Thumb beat/drumbeat stops. "Let's just say his legacy is murky."

"You believe it?"

"Doesn't matter what I believe. Director Harker's the true believer. 'Course your father's penny's still in the pot. Either you and I or Harker's going to claim it. Want first shot?"

HAL RETRIEVED HIS SIG from the hall drawer. Drexler asked if he'd drive. "Easier for you to find your own car." And easier for Morton Drexler to devour the rest of the sandwich he picked up off the floor before they went along.

"Why do you keep a safe house around here?"

"I'm serious about your father." Some lip-smacking of queso. "Much as you want to put your head in the sand, Captain, you've put it in an anthill."

Because his heart was true and pure, Hal could not conceive of his father as treasonous. Furious with Silas since July, he'd warned him that this dead/divorce/Gwen-cash bullshit over Michael would compromise his career. His honor. His family. And wreck his legal entitlement and liberty to it. But this wasn't about Hal. This windup was for leverage against Silas.

A quick two highway exits on-off and they were in Old Town.

"You know I won't compromise my father. You can't possibly think, if I discover anything on Silas, I won't make sure it's hidden from your fat ass even better."

"Spare me. Hal, you're a soldier. You operate covert, but you're not a spy. Of all the Kingstons, you chose a profession of integrity over the profession of deceit. And I'll go you one further. You let your father twist your arm to help him protect Michael's girls from that piece of work that's your sister-in-law, and that's eating you up."

Hal shot him a look. Stared.

"Eyes on the road. I don't know everything. Just enough. You'll protect those girls if Silas says so, but your sons are going to carry the Kingston name. With nobility. At the end of the day, *your* family is going to come first."

Hal gripped the wheel.

"Look at it from my point of view, captain. If I do this outside your family—without you—even with Harker driving it, it will always appear my sour grapes vendetta against your dad. I put you on it? I *expect* you to work your hardest to prove me wrong. Save everyone but Harker's reputation, all I care. If you can't, you're the one Kingston—the only Kingston—who won't betray the truth. That kind of lie would be too big for you."

"Why not Lynn? She hates Silas. She'd go at this like a pit bull."

"Her habits, shall we say, preclude her credibility."

"She's sober."

"Only because she's had a hole in her throat."

Drexler finished the sandwich. Used the moist wrapper as an ineffective napkin.

"But for blood, you and I aren't all that different. We've spent life answering Silas's every whim. What he asked you to do—while for the good of your brother's family—comes at the cost of every single thing you hold sacred. He made you sell cheap. Like me, he found you disposable." Drexler balled the wrapper. Tossed it in the back. "Your sister as well. You already took down one of the three from the crew who almost took her."

"Dulles? That's impossible."

"From all points of human decency, but Dulles *is* KALEIDOSCOPE. You just saw the photo of Houton's

hitters. This camp I want to get you into: KALEID-
SCOPE.

"Hal, do you know what happened to Mr. Edward Lee
Howard?"

Hal found Melody's big red Dodge Ram. Pulled up
parallel on the dark Halloween street.

"You said it. He's the one that got away. Defected to
his Soviet masters."

"KGB gave him a dacha. Didn't have any windows
high enough to throw him out of, so—ten years ago, July
twelfth—he broke his neck on the front steps when he
bent down to pick up his newspaper."

"So what? Soviet Union ended. Russians were done
with him. That's their M-O."

Drexler shrugged. "I don't disagree. But here's the
thing. This Houton connection? I looked back over it.
What do you think I found? All the important parts:
KALEIDOSCOPE restricted. One thing that wasn't?
Houton's personal notes on Howard's daily dacha rou-
tine the week before he died—submitted to your father.
Lot a'questions."

Hal sat and stared. Way out beyond the hood. To
where he couldn't see what was ahead.

"Answers to all what you're thinking might wait for
you in the desert."

Hal lurched out. Waited for Drexler to come around.
Gave his answer. They took an appropriate pause to
acknowledge they weren't about to shake hands.

Hal opened the Ram's door. His words, heavy in the
air between them, sickled on his heart. Surreal. A part of
him didn't believe he'd spoken. Another part urged him
to dial up the yellow phone and lay it out to Silas. Give

him a running chance if he needed it. The genuine part of him knew he'd do none of those things except do the mission—the Iraqi desert or wherever it would take him.

Drexler hit the button running back his seat. Hal shook his head at the man's expansiveness. Fired off a casual afterthought with sniper's precision. "One last thing."

Caught Drexler off guard, a hulking housecat behind the steering wheel. "Aren't we done? What is it?"

Doris reads aloud. I'm in her lap. Michael, Indian style, at her feet. Enrapt. Lynn plays cat's cradle/pretends boredom; I think she listened closest of all. What's it King Arthur says?

"Well, Cap'n? Out with it."

Something like: "If you bring this monstrous accusation forward and fail in its proof, I shall pursue you remorselessly and destroy you."

Way-back-when words to fucking live by.

"Fat or fit, what man aspires to be his own grandma?"

Into the big red truck, he roared into the night.

MORTON DREXLER headed home to Virginia. His Falls Church Greek revival. Laughed at Hal's last crack, and this was the most genuine emotion he exhibited all night. Everything else had been "live your cover." His cover was Harker. What did Harker think, Silas Kingston/KALEIDOSCOPE-wise? What did he feel? Whatever Drexler told him to think. Whatever Drexler made him feel. All Drexler was doing was vamping on an instinct.

Although the fat counterintelligence officer's methods and actions appeared villainous, Silas Kingston had encouraged this behavior in Morton Drexler since the early nineties. When Silas placed young Morton as Meryl Hofmyer's catspaw in the Directorate of Operations where she worked her way up the staff, submarining the wake of the risible Jeremy Harker; when that caustic Teletubby made her move against Harker and into Silas Kingston's division, Silas had already installed Drexler ahead of her to act as Meryl's right hand. Opened the Counterintelligence door for her and dutifully stepped aside. Her gatekeeper. Made sure if the gate came crashing down, it would be Drexler's hand crushed beneath it. Were Drexler judged for courses taken after being played patsy to Silas's invisible move of Ms. Hofmyer to Administrative Secretary OTRAC/KALEIDOSCOPE, judged for courses yet to come as having behaved villainously, Drexler was not a villain. Even Silas, who spoke of Langley as a drafty old castle, would acknowledge to his dying day that Morton Drexler had been, albeit faithless and conniving, one of its most institutionally dedicated and bannered knights.

For all Silas Kingston had done to this fat knight, Morton Drexler wanted disaster to sweep Silas Kingston away. He played every hand to affect this end.

Drexler did not know, could not fathom, how by participating in Silas's disaster, he set himself to take part in his tragedy. To meddle in tragedy brought tragedy upon oneself. For tragedy is not justice, nor is it fate. The nature of tragedy, as opposed to bad luck, to justice, to nefarious machinations, the calamity of catastrophic disaster, or to a random evil, was that it befell all who took part in it.

Drexler fed his cats and tucked himself into bed. Self-satisfied. Warm. Fat and happy, he closed his eyes, while in Moscow, tragedy slipped a different mask over her face.

Her eyes fell upon Michael. The kaleidoscope turned.

4.

L ULU'S FACE GAVE EXPRESSION to the Moscow sky. In Michael's first glimpse, and in every expression rewarded him after—abandoned merriment, hard compassion, bitter delight, sorrow—Ludmila Sidorova's countenance defined for Michael Kingston what the sky over Moscow refused to reveal that fall. It overwhelmed his vision, no matter the direction he looked. Hers was the veiled face of the sun above this authentic and permanent capital of the East. As it defined and lined the city, so too it illuminated his soul.

The Moscow sky. A massive silvery white sheet of zinc met and rising across a critical horizon. Broad cityscape of large buildings. Large streets. Large squares. Large and fanciful churches. A feeling of at once being in an infinity-scape and of being trapped beneath a massive dome, the horizon sealed in all directions.

And the bells.

"I've drunk a little too much tonight, Michael. Take me to bed?"

Her desolation. Her unuttered courage. Her hard compassion to pound his burning spirit into an armor he would wear the remainder of his lifetime. Her tears to oil plating she forged to protect his breast. His heart beat against it inside his chest. Her cherished love: the unuttered tears kissed from his worn and warmed face.

♛ ♛ ♛

"IF YOU BELIEVE LIFE happens at conception, our sparks lit at the same moment from twin flames of destiny's fire."

"That's supposed to make me feel better about this shitshow of my paternity?"

"It was supposed to make you shut the curtains on that shitshow and make you feel better about the big enough shitshow that's simply you."

"And the one that's you?"

"For that, you have the best seat in the house. Birthday neighbors. They say you should never look a gift horse in the eye."

"Is that what they say?"

"Who wouldn't?"

Michael grins and rolls over her and—makeup removed before bed; pink lipstick wiped clean—Michael kisses Lulu's lips, snow white, cinnamon-freckle dusted, moist and eager.

A breath between them.

"Michael. If you stopped? This running. Let go. Stay?"

"And if I said yes?"

♛ ♛ ♛

LUDMILA SIDOROVA was rare. Backwards turn the kaleidoscope. The hidden sun that Moscow fall. Brilliantly flawed like everything her city represented/presented to foreign eyes. First sight of her quivered in Michael a species-centric fear, a primordial neural response to abnormality in others, and because of it, she possessed the rarest beauty Michael would ever encounter. Cherish. Find in Lulu's heart a home he never knew to walk inside.

They had their first conversation two weeks after Dr. Kiselyov identified her as Pinwheel's daughter and his probable cutout. He had followed her every day and every night since. She finally made the approach, storming right up to him.

"Ms. Sidorova, I'll stop haunting you right now if you tell me you don't know why I am."

She laughed in his face. "Those bodyguards, getting jumping over there—"

"Jumpy?"

She didn't smile. "They'd like to make sure you never walk again."

Snow-promised wind ran fingers through fox fur around her collar. Tickled the sharp line of her snow-white jaw.

"If you tell me you don't have something from your father to give to me, I will walk away."

Disdain. "A man does not wait on a woman's approach. You, too much a boy. A boy scuffing toes on sidewalks, moping on benches, following in taxi cabs, drinking alone at disco bars with your sad dog face. A Russian man wouldn't cower from bodyguards and pine."

"Who's cowering?"

"A Russian man would walk to my face and initiate the conversation weeks ago. He'd have balls Americans—"

a broad up-down measure of him with her eyes— "like you, do not."

Disdain to open scorn. Hard to accomplish with eyes of a woodland fawn. Michael chuckled inside; couldn't tell her his boyish crush, his ludicrous fear of dismissal—not violence—had driven the man he thought he'd always been into hiding behind the boy he'd embarrassingly become. Michael hung a curled lip on his hangdog face. While the man inside remembered his long ago business cards—

Culture is YOU. America supports it. Call me. Pleased to meet. Happy to talk.

—the boy he'd let himself become, crossed his eyes.

Her laughter mocked both versions of him a fool. "At lunch tomorrow, they open the Victor Vasnetsov Museum for me. I take a private viewing."

"What time is lunch?"

"Look it up."

"Then it's a date?"

"You? No chance." She whipped around, a practiced move that caused the twin ropes of her snow-hair braids to lash his chest and face. The younger of the two bodyguards beside her black Maybach 57, feinted at him. Michael played along. Feigned fright. The older bodyguard, almost as pale as Ludmila, features sharp, with brown hair that, once determined to be red but having failed, stood out in age like honey on an old bear's head who's stuck his face in a beehive; the older bodyguard smiled. Cold and grim. Doesn't give a sniff how many bees sting him. Around this old bear, every bee possesses one common quality. Every stinging bee ends up dead.

Michael rubbed his cheek where the black gold wedding band at the end of the braid struck him. His fingers came away bloody. He didn't mind it at all.

♔ ♔ ♔

THAT DAY FOR LUNCH, Michael shared Dr. Dosifey Kiselyov's meal. A creamy, flour-thickened, peppered mushroom and potato soup.

"What are these, chanterelles? Bella mushrooms?"

"*Lisichki.*"

♔ ♔ ♔

TURN THE KALEIDOSCOPE. After the doctor's participation in Kalaydoskop's operation to reveal the Russian spymaster's part in Michael's strange birth, Dr. Kiselyov was adamant Michael disclude him from any further enterprise espionage. "Operations, activities, all-dagger-no-cloak pursuits. I'll have none of it. I'm happy, free, and I am alive, thank you very much. My debt to you and your mother is paid. I want you out by end-of-day-tomorrow-goodbye!"

That was the day after Halloween. He stuffed the Aeroflot ticket and diplomatic pass into Michael's hand. "I'll advise you again to use this. None of the other will bring you anything good." He hammered the air with his celery stalk of a finger at the documents.

Michael tapped his foot. Considered the ticket. Tapped his foot. Considered the diplomatic pass. He didn't have to pursue Kolya Yurenev any further. Didn't have to prove to himself, or not, that the Russian was his biological father. Didn't have to entangle anymore in the web that spymaster spun around him. His foot stopped tapping.

"You're right, Doc." Kiselyov's finger-stalk stopped hammering. "I don't have anything to pack. Might as well go now."

Michael made for the door. Gripped the handle. Glanced over his shoulder. Gave a patient smile.

"What? What else?" Dr. Kiselyov grumbled, taken by surprise by his patient's easy acquiescence.

"Just curious." Michael cocked his head at the boxes of Soviet secrets/KGB records/photos/phone-tap-tapes and transcripts that filled the spare room where Michael had recuperated. "Now that they're open, you safe with those here? You all by your lonesome?"

Kiselyov screwed his tiny cranberry lips together. Shrugged ponderous shoulders to disguise the niggling tingle in his spine.

Michael shrugged broadly back. Opened the door. Took one step.

Stopped again.

Didn't look back. "Just saying, without me, wrong person comes along, your story might not be the easiest to explain."

♛ ♛ ♛

THE SOUP. The lunch. The mushrooms. The sting on Michael's cheek where Lulu hit him with his own wedding ring.

"I mean, in English. The name we'd call the mush-rooms in America."

"Neither of those two names is American. French. Italian. Not English. *Lisichki.*"

"Whatever. I wanted to give you a compliment."

The doctor chewed dramatically and stared at him with his walnut-shelled eyes. It was now the third week of November and the only comment the goblin man ever made to the issue of their cohabitation was an oft repeated, "The problem with you is you are worse than furniture because you move about. A dog is more useful than you."

"A dog would be just as underfoot. If not more."

"A dog wags its tail because it can see when it's sup-posed to be happy."

"Dogs aren't grateful. I am."

"Dogs are *thankful.*"

"There's a difference?"

"In Russian language— Yes, there is a difference."

"I wouldn't know."

"Don't fool yourself. Your Russian is fluent."

"I wouldn't know about—"

"What wouldn't you know?! You're speaking Russian!"

"I wouldn't know about dogs. I grew up on a big farm. They were forbidden."

"Your sniveling childhood—not my problem. I am a—"

The doctor's soup spoon dribbled halfway to his mouth, annoying him. Michael finished his sentence. "You're a medical doctor. Not a psychiatrist."

"I am a medical doctor. I am not a psychiatrist. Which, the more you pick at this narcissistic scab in your brain, the more you need one."

Michael ate soup. A stretch to be accused of narcissism by the man whose revelations had shattered Michael's identity. "All I wanted was your opinion on her bodyguards."

"I told you what I know. She's the oligarch's widow. Her father sent the boxes. You talk to her tomorrow and have her remove them. Sticking your nose where you don't have to. You are too old to play Romeo and Korableva."

"Who?"

"Chopped up her husband with an axe."

"In Shakespeare?"

"Puh! In Tolstoy."

Although Ludmila Sidorova was a widow, she hadn't chopped up anyone. But Dr. Kiselyov was a man who met his prime at a time when gossip substituted for the news. Oftentimes, more truthfully. When the doctor had matched his birth record of Pinwheel's daughter with the well-known and mysterious widow Ludmila Sidorova, Michael knew that Kiselyov devoured his quest for her as much as he consumed the Russian-dubbed Mexican soap operas playing all day on his television.

Gossip, still better than the news in Moscow. They continued, silent, with their soup. The TV babble crescendoed with Mexican passion.

"Why do you play that stuff all day?"

"Some people pray to the thin air to be close to their departed loved ones; these were my wife's religion. I spend my days with her saints and sinners in their Mexico City high-rise. Makes me feel closer. It's my religion."

They stared at each other across their bowls. They both knew Michael's pursuit of Ludmila Sidorova was more than a fallen spy's quest for intelligence. Michael crept back up on the question of the bodyguards.

"Instead of whisking her into her car, removing her back to her Presnensky penthouse, they allowed her to engage me. Engage in conversation without listening in. Must say, she didn't behave like any kind of prisoner to me."

Kiselyov lit a cigarette. Allowed himself one, daily. "After your scene last night at the disco where she murdered her husband—"

She didn't axe-murder him, but questions lingered.

"Yeah. Didn't seem all that broken up. Lulu was *living* it up. *Dancing* on his grave, so to speak. Three nights in a row."

Turn the kaleidoscope. Дискотека часовня опасная...

...DISCO CHAPEL PERILOUS. The first night. Lulu arrived on the scene at 11:30. Curb space ready-cleared for the Maybach 57. The surging line behind the velvet rope backed up ten feet, threatened by a pair of granite bouncers while the nightclub's chief of security, the largest boulder of the bunch, unhooked a rope that fronted silver draperies glimmering gray and black with the threaded silhouette of the Ural Mountains.

The pitch-black hole of the vestibule behind, scatter-shot with colored laser light, mirror ball cast reflection. A small red-tuxedoed manager, whose wild hair and Rasputin beard were, together, three times the volume and size of his twitchy skull, spread arms which appeared to marionette his lips into a smile.

Lulu's Chechen opened the backseat door. Lulu dressed in black and white; a chessboard melted into an alternating dazzle of female glamor and allure. She led with her go-go boots and her legs kept coming. The surging crowd of hopeful/potential patrons went still as one. Still as bunched cats with hungry eyes on a resting bird, one pounce short of desire when the invisible gives their bird flight. Lulu glided across the red carpet and vanished within. The line surged; they caterwauled and clawed for cream.

"If you do something like this more than once—" Michael's taxi driver jerked his chin at the Maybach, more bodyguards jumping out of a follow car, two of them already looking Michael's way— "you end up dead."

Michael paid up. Was getting out.

"Maybe even once, if you plan to follow her inside."

"What can I say? I'm mad for dancing."

That first night, Michael was refused admittance.

The second night, Michael was refused admittance.

Third night, same.

The disco closed during the week.

Friday night, the second week, Michael arrived early. First cat—or was it bird? —at the rope. The stony bouncers recognized him. Communicated with loud eyes from stone faces that his presence put him in avalanche danger. There was no *if* in their looks. Just *when*, and *crushing ain't pretty*. But early put Michael up against the velvet rope. Early put him as close as he had yet been to the princess. The prisoner. The Lulu of it all. A whirlwind in a sheath of green and purple sequins. Snow-hair, Medusa-coiled around her skull.

Michael spent an hour bypassed by curious cats ushered through. No doing anything about it. Nearing 1 a.m. A lull. The rope-rock took a breath. Took a beat to crack his neck.

Michael spoke for the first time. "Always on the wrong side of every door."

But for his flawless Russian, the crusher would have ignored him. "You a guy thirsty for pain."

"I am thirsty." He slipped his black gold wedding band from his finger. "This is eighteen karat black gold. Easily worth fifteen hundred US."

The security chief stepped over. Took the ring. Looked for, found the stamp. English: "Bar only. Talk okay. Flirt, not okay. Touch gets you pain. No Lulu. No dance."

Michael nodded. Offered a handshake. Received an open-palmed hammer-clutch to his shoulder. Another hard look. The rope lifted. A shove through the Ural mountains of glittering thread.

A bar. A high stool. A bartender. Michael: "Moscow Mule." Blank look. "Vodka, ginger beer, copper mug? Maybe these parts we just call it a Mule?"

A bar man grin. "Vodka Buck."

Got one. Paid and doubled down with his tip.

A DJ in shiny canvas clown-suit pajamas, Elton John big-bead glasses. Derivative Russian millennium electronica overdubbed with a spectacular blend of Russian pop female vocalists dueled a scratchy, 1960s all-male, trudging woodcutter folk song platter.

Lulu loved the music. Everyone loved Lulu. In turn, she took them as partners. Men. Women. Single and in pairs. It seemed to Michael a choreography; all knew where to be, when to lean, to circle, touch, and where and when to part, swallowed back into the crowd.

Lulu loved the dance. When alone, she dominated the center of the floor. Caressed by swirling spots; pinpointing and surrounding; busting apart, bursting in distinct shards, cartwheeling shafts. Wide bars of light. Bars flung wide as her arms—widespread and taut. Lulu twirled serene and mad and hypnotic. Hands supple. Fingers drooping. Undulating. Leaves at the ends of lissome birch boughs in slow, soft, summer breeze. Her chin tilted upward. Music rose from her throat into the sweaty air to fill the hall.

She sang a note. A single tone.

Pitched to the DJ clown's spin. A trumpet-toned octave above the song now enslaved to her, and because it was true, so true, pure and sad, it sought the hollow space of Michael's guilt—guilt over things he had nothing to do with except for the psychic betrayal of thought, betrayal of being, betrayal of why—and when Lulu ended her exultant note, Lulu spun. Exhilarant green and purple like a hard-flung child's spinning top.

Received another lucky partner. Spinning together; cast aside.

Another lucky partner. Spinning together and cast aside.

Another lucky partner spun and cast, and Michael felt, in all of it: longing like he had never grasped but had always known.

Lulu's fingers. Delicate. Drooping.

Undulating like leaves in summer's breeze.

A small and leafy town. You know it's out there.

Wish your whole life for its pleasant, dreamy, warm-misted streets.

A town no one has ever found.

Until you have.

This moment.

This now.

Lulu.

♕ ♕ ♕

MORNING CHURCH BELLS carried Michael into Dr. Kise-lyov's apartment. Tolled/counted hours until Saturday night.

3,500 rubles. A bit over one hundred US. All it took.

Michael followed his special rules. Bar/vodka buck/no flirt.

Lulu arrived. A hood and tunic of a thousand fine, golden noodle chains. The music, the lights, the dance.

The morning bells continued throughout the entirety of Sunday.

Sunday night. Line long. A party chasing the flee-ing/fleeting feet of the weekend. Michael singled out. Signaled to the front. Rubles out. None accepted.

Nervous at the bar. The lights, different. No flash. No laser. Music subdued; DJ Clown spinning cloying day-spa hypnosis. Huddled dancers edged the floor and swayed. Color expanded the air; a watercolor painter's palette diffused. Noticed something unnoticed on his way inside: cheap easels, black cardboard posterboard, retro black-and-white glossies of a retro monkish youth.

Lulu arrived at midnight. Lulu wore a pale blue, off shoulder, mermaid hemmed 1960s circa-last-week evening gown. Grace Kelly gloves to Lulu's elbows. On Lulu's arm, the young monk from the photographs. Lulu walked around the dance floor. Instead of dancing, Lulu took a love seat near the DJ booth. Nodded to DJ Clown.

Techno-furious, teeth-vibrating music attacked. The night's monkish main attraction received Lulu's kiss. Walked to the turntable dais. Someone pulled the curtain behind the Prince Valiant coifed monk. A spotlight exploded white, gleamed three graduated bell stands. Church bells the young monk played as if in the highest domed-and-storked tower in all of Russia. Unlike a carillon tuned for melody, his bells, like all Russian bells, were cast for atonal harmony. The monk's hands danced between clappers. His polyrhythmic sequences emphasized complex patterns of matching timbre that flowed through the industrial electro-narcotic noise. Michael, trapped in his astonishment, heard in each ring—

Lulu. Lulu. Lulu.

Michael had arrived in Moscow in crisis. Fever. Full mental/physical breakdown. Dr. Kiselyov's care restored his physical health. Saved his life. But in this thunderous tintinnabulation, the shackles that had enthralled his mind broke. Cascaded from his soul. He did not see her approach. Felt only her hand upon his forearm.

"This shit sucks. Want to get out of here?" She was gorgeous. "I know a place—hotter than this on its best night." She wore a yellow vinyl mini dress that looked an awful lot like a little boy's fireman costume. It was. "Champagne bottle service with Cristal," she purred, leaning into his ear.

She wasn't Lulu.

She was an invitation to pain. Destruction from the two no-flirt Stonehenge bouncers with *We fucking warned you!* eyes cascading toward him.

"No. Sorry, hun. Get lost." Michael pushed back his surfer hair with both his hands. Clear eyes, full heart. "Quick, now." Pays to be ready for a beating.

She looked. She saw. She squealed. But then a funny thing happened. Across the floor, Lulu, mesmerized by her bell-ringing monk, did not look at Michael. She touched her Chechen's hand. His eyes leapt to the bouncers. Eyes deadly. The bouncers stopped like cartoon bullies skidding on smoke-throwing heels.

Next day. Outside the luxury shops on Stoleshnikov Lane. With hair bullwhips, Ludmila Sidorova hit Michael's cheek, his own wedding ring drawing blood on his face, and smote, he was smitten.

♔ ♔ ♔

BOTH MEN, EMPTY SOUP BOWLS. The doctor waved out his wooden match like a magic wand that worked backwards which, Michael thought—fire vanishing—matchsticks surely were. Though magic, they carried the exact opposite of surprise in their extinguishment.

"It's the older one. So the gossip goes. The Chechen. Once in the services with Kolya and the one known as Pinwheel, her father, R-I-P. He went into the personal services. For twenty years, served as Princess Lulu's husband, Maxim's bodyguard."

"And the gossip?"

"The Chechen helped her husband, Maxim, off that rooftop and she went from princess to prisoner. Or so they say."

Michael stood. Leaned in. Collected the soup bowls. The doctor made a gesture with the fire end of his cigarette close to Michael's wounded cheek.

"Did the Lulu bite you?"

Michael placed the dishes with a clatter into the sink. "Pretty much. And for your information, it isn't French, it's Latin, so Americans call chanterelles the same damn thing as everyone else. Except ass-backward *Lisichki*-shit Russians."

"You're playing with fire."

"How Kingstons have been preparing for the afterlife since we arrived on the scene. Excellent soup, Doc. Thanks."

Dr. Kiselyov grunted. Smoked. Frowned at the wall as Mexicans argued from the box in his sitting room before throwing each other on a bed.

"And remember, tell her to remove the damn boxes. I want them gone."

But Michael didn't have to tell Lulu. Both men awakened the next morning to an opposite of Christmas. Boxes/files/evidence of Silas Kingston's lifelong treason against the United States: wrapped up, sacked, vanished.

"Windows. Doors. All still locked from the inside. Unless one of us is lying; assisted them…"

Both men knew the other hadn't. Michael offered. "Midgets down the chimney?"

"You'd be surprised. They left the airplane ticket: take it and go home."

♛ ♛ ♛

THE SPY WITHOUT ORDER, without commission, the spy without license, adrift of any law, the disruptor in the shadows: Michael. His cover, worse than compromised, blown of all value to dust. Written off and blotted out. He was not stupid. Michael Kingston could appreciate why the Russian security services let him escape the mental hospital outside of Tula. Let him stumble to Moscow. Let him recuperate with Dr. Kiselyov and read his father's treason. Could appreciate why Kolya/Kalaydoskop offered him a free ticket out, and when Michael didn't take it, let him stalk an assassinated oligarch's strange widow for weeks. Michael wasn't stupid. Nikoláj Yurenev/Kolya/Kalaydoskop decreed all this and incontestably maintained the power to enforce his will. Michael was being enticed. Manipulated. Recruited. Being run.

What of his own agency? Lynn had tried to bring him back. Twice. On/off the books. After that, with the murder of Helene hunting/haunting him, CIA procedure dictated intervention. Secure. Debrief. A measure of accounting. Accountability; some form of professional judgment. Langley had his number; knew he was operational without orders. Instead, CIA clandestine officer Michael Kingston found himself erased. Because they knew and did nothing—toiled to forget him/vanish him—Michael accepted that whatever he did/was doing/would do, the Agency didn't give a shit.

Compass smashed.

True God-aimed north—which on the CIA shield points to the truculent eagle that mounts it; vigilant eyes unflinching—lost of all magnetism, spun out, dangled/broken, and still.

FOR CLOSE TO SEVENTY YEARS, the Soviet Union maintained/enforced an unofficial position of atheism. Of churches—some torn down, some shuttered, some left dormant. Most repurposed to communist utility. Most notable: Red Square's famous and picturesque St. Basil's Cathedral converted into a State Historical Museum. Of architecture, history, politics. The myth of religion. Those few churches left for the practice of faith, were left only to gather the names of those who dared enter. Those with nothing left to lose.

But there were churches now. Holy-GD-whoa! Boards torn from windows, doors thrown wide, the communist converted re-re-purposed back to Christianity with the hammering of nails, the hammering of bells; of churches— *"Doc, what's with the incessant bells? My God."*—there were now somewhere between 600 and 800 orthodox temples, churches, cloisters, and chapels in Moscow. Each had a faithful crew of bell ringers like Lulu's artist from Sunday night, who had over one hundred reasons to beat the clappers, and another score or two of improvised seasonal tollings and their reverberant bombilations—

"You expect something else? Michael, Christmas is coming."

"It's November. You people don't celebrate Christmas until January. This is worse than the frickin' department stores!"

Michael got over it. The bells. The hangover. Asked, "So many churches—did everyone worship in secret?"

"Fool. Whose heart is a secret to God?"

Michael finished his coffee. Three hours early, he left the doctor's apartment to run a habitual/unnecessary SDR. Get a jump on his art museum meet. It was after seven in the morning. The bells, rung every hour, now temporarily silent. After his religion-in-Moscow lesson with Kiselyov, Michael suddenly noticed seven churches just on his way to the neighborhood metro.

Tucked between apartments and businesses, public buildings and play parks, their clustered domes reminded him of mushrooms sprung up from dry and thirsty earth after an unexpected rain. He didn't know why Russians put domes only on their churches, but maybe, as he did, they found their inspiration in their peculiar sky. That heavenly illusion Michael never experienced before Moscow. Sky as entrapping bell jar, mankind as a specimen. He moved on foot through morning traffic. Pedestrian to-ing and fro-ing. Stair-stepped blocks. Dog-legged down. And back. The pauses and the chokepoints. A spy's "direct" path toward the Metro station.

In Moscow, unlike New York, or London, Paris, Rome, the "urgent business" vibe coursing like an uninterrupted/uninterruptible tide in every direction did not exist. Neither did the Western style of loitering or take-a-break surrender to the day. Everything doing, even not-doing in Moscow, was done with solemn determination. And no one's determination pushed its value over anyone else's. Street sweeper, banker, shopper, government official, pensioner, doctor, student, worker: a shared equality of purpose demanded of themselves and from each other.

No one on the streets of Moscow ever did nothing.

Because of the city's vast perspectives, its citizens appeared to function in a constant state of preparation; to Michael Moscow appeared as though the city waited for more people to arrive. The idea amused Michael as he clambered down the Metro stairs. He imagined similar ideas burrowing into the brains of Hitler. Of Napoleon. The Teutonic Knights. The Mongols. He waited, two trains, eyes keen for surveillants before he boarded onto the Lyublinsko-Dmitrovskaya line. Headed for the Meshchansky District. Rode to Dostoevskaya station.

Named after Fyodor Dostoevsky, born in a hospital above the station stop, its beige marble walls and columns were inlaid with gray/black/white marble mosaics. Stark in their depictions of scenes from *The Idiot*. From *Crime and Punishment.*

Michael left his car. Stood face to face with Svidrigailov. Marble chip eyes met Michael's living gaze. The moment the dissolute villain puts the bullet in his head.

Tore himself away. Round the column. Into the moment Raskolnikov murders Alyona with the axe. From the end of the platform—the largest mosaic of all—the author's face, stern and brooding, thrust outward from the stone. Bore into Michael with vicious warning/judgment/fury. Permanent and implacable. It gave expression to everything held buried beneath the Russian soil. Russian soul. Michael ducked his head. Avoided the author's following gaze. Jogged up the escalator. It was snowing and much colder on the surface than when he'd first stepped outside. The dome closed around him like a plastic bag tightened over his head.

5.

THE VICTOR VASNETSOV HOUSE met the landscape as if dropped from a flying carpet between block apartments and anonymous industrial concrete. Green wooden gates. Wooden arched gateway. Spear-topped posts. A wooden turret loomed fancifully from the red/white checkerboard barrel roof Michael glimpsed over the shoulder of the security guard who greeted him— "Mikhail Nikolaevich." Michael Son of Nikoláj.

Nothing like being mocked to prove you're wanted.

"Not a certainty, but if the lady requires, I'll say 'yes.'"

The look of a Christmas nutcracker. No hint he heard/listened/cared. His wooden jaw clapped, "This way, sir."

A garden path presented the famous folklore artist's home as though it turned on corner legs to meet him. White-plastered stone inlaid with vibrant tiles of colorful flowers. The second-story windows above, done to appear *kokoshiks*—those crenellated, lace-curtained headdresses of 16th century feminine peak popularity—ready for peasant girls' faces to peer out and appear princesses, peered empty. The path curved him around to the ornate and whimsical porch.

What was the one my mother liked? The witch who trapped and ate her visitors...

Delivered to the docent, she in nutcracker matching blue jacket, skirt instead of trousers, smiled like every grandmother in every cookie commercial—

What the hell am I doing here?

She's here. Lulu.

—gestured Michael to the wooden spiraled staircase. A vigorous hand wag when he paused. Wasn't about to go with him.

"Mrs. Sidorova is upstairs?"

"*Ludmila Igorevna* is studying the Seven Fairy Tales."

Michael gripped the wooden banister, smoothed with age by tenderness. "And me. Number Eight."

"Watch your head on the beam, sir."

Halfway up the lazy oval turn, Michael heard humming. Haunting. Melancholic. Minor. His pulse increased to teenage tempo. He entered the turret studio. Took in her braid coils of snow hair, her alabaster cheek in profile, her glacier-colored hands that idled on the honeyed arms of the carved wooden chair she seated. Her idle hands glowed with the vitality of the hottest part of fire. Her birdsong trailed into lyrics—

"Fairy tales I'll start to tell you/Songs I'll sing you too;/Eyes are closing, drift to sleep now,/*Bayushki-bayu*—" trailed off into spoken words— "Do I mystify you? Are you frightened yet?" She looked back. An appraising smile without pleasure. "Are you in love with me or do you find me freakish?"

Michael gave her half of the same smile back. "I think they call it lust. But I'm smart enough to get over that. The other? No. Uh, I take it back. Yes. 'Freakish.' But not the way you think; your condition. You just make a point of acting and talking freaky. Appears to be your best-brightest tease."

"'Go hard or go home.' Isn't that the American idiom?"

"Something like that."

Of all the times he'd seen her, today Lulu was dressed most provocatively unprovocative. Jeans tucked into boots. A loose red chenille sweater. Same fox-collared jacket of yesterday but tied around her waist and scrunched in the chairback behind her, reddish brown fur spilling out the sides.

"I'm to say," she said without turning, "you don't have to take this further."

"Which is a stupid reverse psychology way to get me to keep going."

"Are you? Keeping going?"

"Whatever. What do you have for me?"

She turned her face. Looked at him. "Was he smoking—my father—when you saw him last?"

"My take? Cigarettes weren't something he stopped for any length of a minute. They're not what killed him."

Looked away. "When I knew I'd most likely meet you, I looked you up. Your family, all the way back, made their fortune killing people with tobacco. Is that something you're proud of? Michael?"

A freakish piece a'work.

My Lulu. (Make it so.)

He shaped and discarded half a dozen pithy phrases. Leaned into his annoyance. "I know I don't care." He pointed to a matching chair intricately as carved but in patterns relief to the one she seated. "May I?"

Lulu nodded. Michael eased into the chair.

Her eyes racked. Focus from him to focus inside herself. "Live by the sword..." Serious: "I have what you want." Normal: "And don't bother me with a lot of questions because I know nothing about what my father and my godfather involved themselves in." Peering back out, a Lulu he'd never seen; the sad Lulu. The woman, he would learn, life had beaten Lulu into hiding. Hiding herself inside her *matryoshka* self, nesting smaller and smaller. "It must have been awful to find out what you found out about your birthday. I'm sorry. It's a very dumb story. Worse, because it is real life."

His lust left him and with it his judgment of her. His clandestine officer's categorizing her into psychological types, dissecting her personality into a set of forms he could build into a useful framework. Or gallows. She was as real as he. And as lost.

"Ludmila—"

"Lulu. Please."

"Lulu. Did you bring what—"

Pinwheel. Kalaydoskop. All bad. All fire. Run.

"—your father entrusted you to give me?"

She looked at his face, taking it for herself, before accepting his eyes. "I have it at home. But I have a request. It has nothing to do with your business. My father's business."

"Espionage? Spying?"

"It may be that, but to me, it is personal. I will ask you to accomplish it as a condition of our exchange."

"That's probably a bad idea."

"It is a terrible idea. And you'll say 'no' when I tell you. And I will have you do it."

"Tell me."

"No. I can't trust you with it. Now. I need to know you better. Here." A white finger touched his breast. "And here."

He watched her finger move from his heart to hers. He said, "I'm not comfortable with this."

"You don't know what 'this' is."

"Whatever it is, help me understand. Did your father or Kolya put you up to this game?"

"No. My father would not approve and my godfather—"

"Kolya."

—a nod. "He would be furious; he must not find out until you two meet—if that's what you decide to do. We are both his prisoners."

"I could just lie to you. About everything. You know that's my line of work. I'm good at it."

"I count on you being the best for what I'll require of you. But the way I've arranged this, it will be entirely impossible for you to lie to me."

With her words, a twinkle sparked her eyes. She made her pale eyebrows dance for him. Swiveled in her chair and indicated the wall of paintings.

"Vasnetsov has other works. More important. Famous works, in other more important, famous museums. These he never sold. He kept them for himself and his family. Here. Their Moscow home. He did a series of paintings he worked on for a decade. 'The Seven Fairy Tales.'"

"I count four."

"Patrons commissioned the other three. More important works; more important museums. These four are special."

The Sleeping Tsarevna, The Frog Princess, The Un-smiling Princess, and *Kaschey the Immortal.* She listed them for Michael; she made her request. He cocked his head at the strangeness of it. She reassured him with that same appraising and pleasureless smile. His father's words came at him.

Lips you only see once in your life—
He throttled the thought.
Bury Doris.
Lulu rose. Lulu said, "I am having a formal dinner party at my place tomorrow night."

"A Thanksgiving party?"

"You can play America if you'd like. You will come."

"I don't have pilgrim attire, and I can't see myself putting on a monkey suit—even if I owned one."

"I can. I've delivered formalwear to your doctor's apartment." Off his furrowed brow, an impish grin. "Nothing freakish. Though a tuxedo, I think, is a costume, no? Come early— Seven? You will like who you meet."

She buttoned and belted her jacket. Its fox curled and cuddled around her throat. Michael turned to the four paintings.

Outfoxed.
He laughed inside. Where laughter can be as loud and as joyful as you want.

"Four paintings. Four princesses. My heart you will find in one of these paintings. When you can tell me which one, and where it is beating—even now, on the canvas—you and I will make our trade, Mikhail Niko-laevich. There is no second chance if you get your first chance wrong."

She is gone but she is still here, like a light remaining, filling the empty spiral staircase, humming her little song.

Taunting me.

*"Think, when bracing for fierce battle,/Of your mother true.../Sleep, my dear, beloved baby/*Bayushki-bayu.*"*

6.

A N EIGHTEEN PLUS A twenty-three. A Paige plus a Clive. That kind of math. Not surprising, after the first time, Halloween night, they didn't share Michael's qualms about giving in to lust. Their emotions/passions/hormones unleashed; they leaned into lust. Lay down with it. Back-seated his car with it—

Not his new motel room. "No way." Paige stuck with that. Didn't know why (though Clive did. Fergus).

—but the family beach. Under the rickety stairs. The river—for half-a-minute—cold, cold, *whoa*-ass-"Let's not try that again"-fucking-cold. The porch. Lots there. Every room they could get into before they were falling out of shirts and sweaters and intimate garments, room-to-rooming the Foxtail Farm manor. (Lotta mirrors, too—for better or for pervy fun/funny worse.) Most days/nights that November. Well, some days they missed out. Some nights. To an outside observer, "What're you talking about 'missed' anything? They did it all night, every night. Like animals."

But it wasn't. It was like people. Young lovers throughout history. And, because they were young, even when they weren't having a go, their passion shimmered off them in rays.

"I'm doing Morgan's whole summer in a month."

"Doesn't the us-of-it mean more than what Morgan gets up to?"

She showed him "yes" with her body and her delight.

The Maryland weather grew colder. They remained sweaty. The shorter days made for longer nights. They named it love. Everyone—except the twins and possibly Leigh—knew and, because Silas silently and weirdly commanded it, let them do as blossomed youth, when in bloom, is quintessentially wont to do.

Not a lot of love stories begun so rumpy-pumpy work out. But there was a subtext to Paige and Clive's affair. The granddaughter/daughter of spies mixing with an agent of a foreign service. That was serious, and it was deadly, and it wasn't a game. They were honest about that. Whispers, only truths, when their heartbeats slackened, and they reached that closer place, past the physical place, where two human beings, and maybe only human beings, can realize how serious this and they had become of life.

Gwen—fled to her condo—condoned the girls remaining at Foxtail Farm, demanded they miss her, and none of her daughters made a peep in argument, fingers crossed behind backs. Gwen's view of her eldest's affair was to—

A: pretend she didn't see it.

B: nurture a burning desire to see Paige hurt Clive. Hard/bad, heart/brain.

Oh, B-plus, too: see Clive teach-a-lesson/crush her overweening Paige out of her weenie-crush. So high-and-mighty that daughter shoving it in her face;

"Paige, honey, I think it's wonderful you two found each other. Forgiveness is so special."

Paige already had "the talk" with Lynn. Preoccupied with work (and—Paige smelled it—drinking again), when Lynn came over in her new Mercedes to discuss Thanksgiving with Melody and go blasting Charlotte and Leigh on a wild ride down their private lane; Lynn looked for Paige's heart in her eyes.

"Remember what we talked about. One time. All it takes."

Later when it all went wrong, their lives destroyed, Paige would recall—collapsed in the guns' thick smoke and the blood's wet stains—that moment, that November day, as *the* moment her subconscious pieced the Lynn/Leigh shards into a recognition of sadness and dishonesty, falsely named sacrifice, as a family truth.

"Remember what we talked about. One time. All it takes." Lynn lifts Leigh—too old for lifting at ten—from her ferocious sports car. Their pieces fit, disguised maternal/manifest filial love complete.

Recalled the natural balance between her aunt and her sister, and because that bond was God's truest form of love, softened Paige's tears that watered their destruction as the dying blood spread around her.

Uncle Hal: pissed at Clive. Pissed at Paige for making him pissed at Clive. Pissed at Silas for allowing Paige and Clive to piss him off. Uncle Hal: pissed about everything these days, but because he wasn't an angry man, or mean, or casually violent, Hal only commented on that fall of their passion with hard/somber disapproving frowns. Glances. Stares. Abandoned of his "only on holidays" rule, he smoked his father's old briars and wind-wafted, watched dawn unveil the river, rising over their inlet bay, and didn't once see the wonder he aways had before. Took the smoke and the nicotine and blew it away. Only coming and going words and not a spoken thought to anyone.

Fine. Melody didn't want to talk about it. She and Hal: mirror images of Paige and Clive not so many years before. Not so many that, surely, Hal hadn't forgotten. Hal's mood disturbed her. Just as Silas had warned it would. Her man, her soul mate, her perfect Hal didn't want to talk about anything at all with Melody since his Halloween disappearance. His midday return, November the first. His scowls at Clive and Paige—antagonistic and stubbornly cold—Melody chalked up less to some moralistic hypocrisy than to his continued dysfunction in their own bedroom.

At night, she curled her toes like the tiny fingers of a pair of hands. Curled them around the toes of Hal's right foot—the one she used to massage her foot against after they made love. In the morning, she worried. Who wouldn't? But Melody kept faith in her heart. Consulted her gut, and it told her to march the Kingstons forward to Thanksgiving, onward to Christmas, blaze the family into new dawn at the coming of the year.

Her stitches came out the middle of the month and her hair grew back. Soft and slow and filling in, framing her sunny charity.

That fall, Melody focused on larger issues. On making her secret something that wasn't. That didn't have to be. A decision to be taken with her father. A decision to be taken with Richmond DA, Calvin Kirby. A decision to be taken with Victoria and with the Kingston past—her family/her past—and how, whatever decisions she made, she would (brace for impact) crash into the future of them all and carry all of them out unscathed.

Melody knew Paige. Knew she'd be careful; having entered the Kingston circle, she felt the person who might need a word was Clive.

A rock-skipping contest on the cold beach. Clive and the twins. She took a minute while Jack and Little Silas searched for a new bucketful of flat, round rocks. The kind that, like God as man, could walk on water.

"You're using protection?"

Jacklit. "Uh— Is it that obvious?"

No need to embarrass him.

"No. Just a woman's sixth sense."

"I am. She is. Both. We do."

Melody nodded. Readied to chase down her twins too far up the beach where the mist felt freer to ensconce and steal.

"May I just say one thing?"

"Clive, of course. Anything."

"I *love* Paige. And don't say something like 'You hardly know her.' Or, 'That makes her heart more breakable.'"

Melody touched his hand. "Opposite. That's what makes hearts strongest of all." The boys returned on their own—

"We got 'em! Excellent ones!"

"Good job!" Clive grinned.

—and Melody finished. "I'm excited for you guys." She moved apart and sat on the driftwood log. Watched the three at play. She pushed at the fog with her being. The fog pulled back.

Of course, it wasn't only an insider's game. There was Fergus. Stomping and growling, guzzling whisky in the stagnated dust and time and permanent dusk of the Garde-Joyeuse. Cans on his ears waiting for a repeat radio intercept that never came. Relying on Clive for a breakthrough. Jealous of the sexcapades. But the room-to-room of it all were his orders. "Find the radio, you'll find the codebook. It's got to be somewhere on the property. Make a fuck-game of it. Just keep opening doors and drawers until you find the bloody thing."

Clive searched. Paige let him, and he told Fergus where he searched and where the codebook wasn't. He created a detailed map of the house. Though, from each room he withheld a key detail. Pretended he didn't notice himself doing it or why. Apart from Fergus, on his own initiative, Clive pressed Paige to get them into Silas's North Vista Outhouse. Get them down to the wine cellar. Get him a look for the Timeless.

Paige knew about the cognac. "Unless you can pick the lock so he can't tell, I'd need Silas's keys, and it's not like I can ask him."

Clive could pick the lock. Something told him not to. Told him the old man would know.

When they weren't going at it, they binge-watched *The Sopranos*. Sometimes with Melody. Sometimes even Hal, even Silas—who sometimes, stunning the rest of them, found it too emotional—and all of them disagreeing on the final ending. Between that and *Friday Night Lights* which Silas didn't watch a minute of and Hal was gone (some training thing that didn't allow an off-base pass), but Melody watched it all. Charlotte and Leigh too. And every episode they'd catch Clive tearing up— "I don't even like American football." Around the television, the Kingstons-plus-Clive felt like a normal family.

Late nights all alone and sweethearting, the lovers binged Alfred Hitchcock. Started at any rate; it ended with *Notorious*.

Paige loved the movie. "The spies, their burning passion for each other, the wine cellar scene—"

She pulled closer. He pulled away.

"Don't you get it? In real life, Cary Grant doesn't stand a chance of saving her. Zero. I can't do this. Do that to you. I gotta go."

And he did. Three days. Then Fergus: "Get your black ass back on her! You don't have a motherfucking choice!"

Three nights later, the Enchanted Forest. Make-up sex. The place Clive refused Paige on her birthday.

"You know, my grandfather isn't going to poison my coffee."

Clive couldn't take her grin. Looked over the crumbled wall of the King's Pavillion. Above the skeletal, swamped jousting knights, ghosts in their raggedy plastic shrouds. Moonlight horizontal across the swampy marsh made silver the heads of cattails rising from the still water like foot soldiers' lances. Clive understood. "You've told him. About me. About everything."

"I didn't. Not everything."

"Don't you see how compromised we are?"

"I didn't tell him *anything*. He told *me*. About *you*."

She held him around his waist. He looked down at her hair in the silver light and Clive believed her because it was true and because they loved each other and knew they wouldn't lie. Not to each other. Never to each other.

(Until they did.)

She caressed his worried face. "If it came down to it, he told me to tell you something." He steadied his gaze on the crown of her head. "Something about your Fergus person."

Clive never mentioned Fergus—not by name. "How does he know Fergus?"

Lifted her face to him. "Silas knows all about him. I think. Sounded like he has for years."

"You never thought to tell me that?"

Her face fell. He touched her face. This wasn't her job. Wasn't her world. Her face broke his heart because with features, love writes more than words can say. "I meant that more as a general question. Not a scold."

Paige nodded. Trusting. Each took a breath. Each steadied the other.

Clive spoke. "I haven't told you. I didn't want to frighten you about Silas. Where this might go."

"I know. He knows."

"I think it's going there. No matter what I find or not."

"Have you heard something? How would you know?"

"In my job—my training emphasized it—there's a shit-ton of paperwork. Log everything. Report everything. Write it up. Dot your I's and cross your T's and file it, file it, file it. There's been the barest minimum on all this—"

"A lot of repetitive pornography, no one wants to—"

"They do. They want it all written down. Except with this, they want as little written down as possible. No accountability."

"I better tell you what Papa told me to say."

"When the time comes. That's what he said, right? Let's trust his timing for what's best for you."

"But—"

"No, Paige. There's something bigger you've told me. It might balance everything out. Might make it all worse." Eyes serious as death. Silas's death. "If he's always known, why did he make that radio call? The one that put me and Fergus onto him?"

"We'd lost my dad. His son. I think…" Her words ran out.

What do I think?

"He's a pro's pro. No one better. He made that call because he wanted Fergus to hear it."

7.

*A*LWAYS THE FALL. THE *time of year known and whispered by slaves as best to escape the Maryland plantations. Longer nights, the cover of darkness increases. Windy, dry, cooler air holds fewer moisture molecules; human scent particles concentrate less. Disperse more rapidly. Unexpected weather changes. Heavy cloudbursts, hurried snow flurries wash out/disguise trails. Don't stick around to kill. And the temperature: not too hot, not too cold, but like Scrapefoot the Fox, escaping the Three Bears Castle, just right for fast travel.*

1678. A Spanish slave from Trinidad, Pedro Kwame, purchased by English Jesuits for their Ignatius Plantation. A 3,000-acre farm, predominately tobacco; dominates the meeting point of the Potomac and St. Mary's River. The purchase of Pedro Kwame—christened Peter Williams—includes a three-year-old boy, claimed/presumed his son. Original name lost to time; christened, Cupid Williams, nicknamed and historically known as Scrapefoot—after the folktale fox who outsmarted those bears long before Goldilocks arrived on the scene to be eaten.

Much like his father, Scrapefoot Williams is inquisitive and inventive; rarely satisfied with the status quo, always seeking improvement, whatever the current state of affairs presented. In the father, these qualities led to Peter's hybridization of Trinidad seed with the tobacco of the Piscataway; with Scrapefoot, well, that kid's just a terror. Instead of hobbling the precocious boy, the priests and the cowled brothers recognize potential in his fertile imagination and budding brains; perhaps, a brighter reflection of his plant-breeder father, they train Scrapefoot as an agriculturalist. The natural sciences appeal to the boy, feed his appetite to push what is *into* what can be. *By age sixteen, Scrapefoot innovations are applied to plantation soil cultivation, in the planting, growing and the harvesting, the curing of tobacco. The St. Ignatius plantation flourishes.*

1693. Competition from quality Maryland tobacco causes Virginia leaf price to plummet. William Digges, son of Edward Digges, former Governor of Virginia and founder of the Virginia colony's largest tobacco farm, E.D. Plantation, attempts to purchase Cupid Williams for the unheard price of 128 pounds sterling. Prayerfully, the priests reject the offer; claim at eighteen, Scrapefoot is too young, Virginia too Protestant, their investment in his soul too valuable. As Scrapefoot's talents and reputation increase, his Jesuit masters reject more lucrative offers from Delaware and North Carolina. By 1696, Scrapefoot Williams is the most valuable slave in the Maryland colony.

In the year of the Lord 1698, in the spirit of Christ, and with Catholic charity, the St. Ignatius priests petition for and receive a ten-mile travel pass in the name of Cupid Scrapefoot Williams from the governor, Colonel Nathaniel Blakiston, allowing the priests to hire out

Scrapefoot to all tobacco growers of Southern Maryland. By 1716, one year into his fourth decade, Scrapefoot enjoys more freedom than any other slave in the colony.

Cupid Scrapefoot Williams, whose scalp and bones will cause much trouble for the son of the original Sylvanus (Silas) Kingston and his slave hunter Turkey John Swan, understands and appreciates his unique situation. His unique freedoms. At age forty-one, he has beaten the average life expectancy of his kind by almost twenty years. He also understands, and he appreciates this more: Fall is the best season in Maryland to make a run for freedom.

November 12, 1716. Scrapefoot runs from St. Ignatius under Thursday's waning crescent thread. On Friday, under the Jesuit promise of one hundred pounds tobacco reward, Turkey John Swan engages in his pursuit and capture. A hand drawn and half-burned map fished out of Scrapefoot's cabin fireplace indicates a typical flight to the fugitive camps that smolder and smoke, warn and dare curses in the wilderness beyond the Monocacy Settlement. One hundred twenty-eight miles to the north.

To the consternation of Scrapefoot's Jesuit masters, Turkey John turns south. "Fool Indian will fall off the point into the bay before he goes ten miles."

New moon. Saturday night. Darkness complete. God's eye shut upon the earth, Turkey John Swan unhitches the mule team from his wagon at the edge of the St. Kitts Forest, a scant five miles from St. Ignatius. Stakes the beasts. Tomahawk, rope, pistols, manacles: gears up, and, these days, this includes a pair of hounds who set to high-pitched hysteria.

The scalphunter doesn't get two steps before Cupid Scrapefoot Williams emerges from the trees. "Will you be wanting my scalp?"

Turkey John balances a hand, top of his tomahawk. Annoyed at the sight of his dogs cavorting around the old slave. Pushing down loose mouthed, loll-tongued heads, Scrapefoot eyes the Native's rope.

"Or you here for my hanging?"

"Less'n there's been a killing. Or rape. A burnin'. You know the fathers don't condone the either."

"Maybe I have."

Too easy. His attitude wrong. Turkey John's eyes search for a weapon. None. "You haven't and you know it. Don't appears you broken a sweat a t'all."

"Want me to hitch your mules?"

"I'll do it." *Never takes his gaze off Scrapefoot as he collects the beasts.* "You will be whipped. Wear irons till you learn. What do you want? I don't make a deal."

"You're known to kill for pleasure."

"When it's in my right."

"Justice?"

"God's and law."

"Is slavery God's justice?"

"It's in the Book. Jesus does not condemn it."

"He don't condone it none. The Gospels speak of the sin of owning people as property."

"Get in the wagon, neger, or you'll be God's property left to rot. I will have your scalp."

Perfectly serene, Scrapefoot Williams climbs onto the wagon. Turkey John slaps about in frustration, putting the mules back in their traces. Smacks their heads, necks, flanks as they nip and struggle against his displeasure.

From the board seat. "How many's it now? You've left to rot. One dozen? Nearer twenty?"

Turkey John Swan's skin prickles. Doesn't turn around. "Eighteen. Four were women. Two were children. Don't push me, neger."

"Them didn't commit no murder. Didn't burn no barns. Didn't rape no one." His next words come, a rapier point driven into Turkey John's breast. "My whipping will heal. The irons come off. I'll run again. And again, till they sell me and I'll run again from there until it's time you hang me or you come back with my scalp."

The scalphunter pulls himself onto the slat bench beside the slave. Shoves his hounds—fast friends with the runaway—into the bed. Barks at them in his Algonquin language. Grabs his reins. Glares at his mule's twitchy ears. "Out with it."

Scrapefoot says, "I've come to a careful conclusion. You and I possess what I 'magine, are similar needs. Deeper than we can explain. Needs we must act upon. Where's in your work you can, in my'n I cannot. But I can feed your dark and secret soul."

Turkey John fights an urge to put a pistol ball through this brazen slave's skull. Whips his straps around the rein hitch. Seizes the slave by the obscenely clean front of his shirt. Yanks him into his face with both hands. "What is it you think you know?"

"That 'tween now and my reward, t'will be me that done delivers you heads for your bloody scalps. More'n you and your master—oh I's sorry—partner, Sylvanus Kingston's pred'lections call."

Friday, November Sixteenth

1.

MELODY DID NOT MAKE good on her vague promise to telephone Victoria Samuels. A few days, and Victoria brought out an old Patuxent Historical Society Donor Directory. A finger down the *K's. Doris Kingston, Foxtail Farm.* Called the number before she chickened out. Chickened out when an older man answered.

A good mystery intrigued Victoria; the odd, frumpy young curator believed this mystery—Turkey John Swan, Sylvanus Kingston, The Case of the Counterfeit Scalp—promised thrilling revelations. Unexpected justice, or a darker/secret opposite, revealed.

Four times over the next ten days, Victoria opened her device. Tapped the Foxtail Farm digits. Hovered her finger over the green icon: Each time, Victoria Samuels did nothing. Phone off. Let life go on.

On second, third, a bunch of thoughts tracked back—fingered through like not finding the right candy or nut or a lucky coin—decided she couldn't have picked a worse way to force a friendship. Melody had skin in the game. Two ways. Literally. Was it a racial thing? Was she subconsciously/subliminally as gross as her father? She fretted that; the way lonely people fret the wrong thing. Always. Second guess dissatisfaction to remain alone.

Life went on and the blatancy of her work kept Victoria's loneliness subdued in accustomed boredom.

👑👑👑👑

TWO HUNDRED AND NINETY-SIX YEARS and two days since the unrecorded meeting of Turkey John Swan and Cupid Scrapefoot Williams. Six days before Thanksgiving. Morning of November the sixteenth, Melody Kingston entered the Colonel Vickery House/Patuxent Historical Society. Displayed polite unfamiliarity in response to Victoria's startled greeting. Even keel. Not off-putting, but not friendly. Just even. Requested the director. Victoria blinked. Her smile shrunk. Melody studied nineteenth century lithography on the walls until Victoria returned with a matron built and colored—her dress, her hair—like a blue heron. Severe of eye; outward calm. A tall bird, almost five feet, made for a short Mrs. Shelly.

"Yes, yes, Mrs. Kingston. I'd recognize you anywhere. A pleasant surprise. Please come right this way into my office. Coffee?"

"Black, please."

"Victoria?" As in, *chop-chop.*

The handshake. Director's choice—desk/coffee table; measures Melody for intent— "You have the settee. Last year, donor generosity allowed us to replicate the original upholstery pattern. I hope you find it comfortable. Everyone does."

Coffee delivered; Victoria ghost/gone.

Down to it. The weather. The holidays; "We have the best carolers for our Christmas tours. Which you must join us. Divine." Rare history, the region, and their shared place in the space and time as custodians and preservationists. Of something non-specific or specifically something implied.

"Your mother-in-law, rest her soul, and her mother-in-law before that, so interested. Gracious ladies."

Melody got/got-to the point. "The Society takes credit card donations?"

"Could, yes. It has. Would. Certainly-and-thank-you."

Melody opened her handbag. "I have a stipulation."

"I see?" She didn't.

"Yes. I'm doing a genealogy." Direct look. "For my father-in-law, Silas Kingston. If your assistant—" Head tilt the door; Victoria beyond.

"Victoria Samuels? She is our *curator*." The matron shifted her hips as though she had gas. "The size? Of your donation."

Three hundred? No. Better five hundred—there goes half of Christmas— That do it?

Melody met the director's acquisitive smile with her American Express. "Six hundred and fifty dollars."

♛ ♛ ♛

WHITE COTTON GLOVES. Hands clasped and resting on the high-gloss library table surface. Melody, eyes shut, searching peace within. Eyelids parted at the dull stutter of a wonky wheel on a pushcart. Two-level; brimming boxes filled both trays. Victoria stopped across from her.

Moved chairs to make room for the cart. Managed not to meet Melody's avid gaze.

"I never reshelved them. Added more, but..." Diffident, probing. "I'd given up you were coming back."

"I'd given up, too." She vaulted Victoria's hesitancy. "Ever since Halloween, there's a side of me that's outrage. A side of me that's guilt. Neither of them allowed me to look at this with unbiased eyes. And why? Because it's slavery. It's original. It's murders and tortures and executions and, you're right, you let it flash in your face and it's the worst crime story in history."

"You called it a serial killer mystery."

"I think you said 'mystery,' but that's what's hung me up and why wouldn't it? That's what these people saw—even before they had a name for it—they thought it, and recorded, and didn't care to do anything other than that."

Melody found herself standing. Victoria awkwardly bowed for her to sit and demonstrated by taking an opposite chair.

"It overwhelmed me."

"It is overwhelming."

Melody zeroed in. Reason she was there: "I didn't see the pieces that didn't fit."

It's not nice to say, but Victoria's was the same thunderstruck and exuberant look a dog gets when it realizes a treat revealed in an open, outstretched hand.

"Like the counterfeit scalp."

"I need you to walk me through that, but more. What I already looked at. Was incapable of seeing."

Second nature, Victoria slipped on cotton gloves. Centered a yellow pad. Clicked a pen. Drawn by

Melody's passion into the calm center of her professional element. "I like what you're saying. Taking notes. Keep going?"

"It's larger. The wharf house. Customs shed. The ledger." Victoria knew it. Nodded. Encouraged. "The ledgers with the numbers of lost/dead slaves with his initials."

"T-J-S. Turkey John Swan."

"When it's losses, those initials continue as some kind of system, I don't know, categorizing, long—like two hundred years—after he's dead. And then, there's the 'Wanted' bills. Marked 'Rendered" and 'Rendered Unto God.'"

"I've gone through those. They match with deaths. It's reasonable. The word 'rendering' as it applies to animal carcasses goes back at least to the seventeenth century."

"That's not my argument. I'm coming at it from the same place. If they both mean the same thing, why are some one and some the other?"

"A religious component?"

"There isn't one. Nothing I read had any religious component. No priest or minister or any prayer. No special reference to religion in burial or disposal. They *are* the same, yet Turkey John Swan and those who followed him, working with the Kingstons—this is all *Kingston* material I've looked at, right?"

Victoria's eyes gleamed. "Yes. This is interesting. Keep going."

"I don't know where to go, just that the difference was there for some Kingston following after who knew what it meant to understand it. That difference."

"Like a message."

Melody teethed her bottom lip. What she'd been building up to. Since her talk with Silas. A kind of Silas moment. Everything—reality/fantasy—hinged on her next word and, briefly, she was afraid to say it.

"A secret. All this stuff is a Kingston code."

"Like secret writing?"

She noticed Victoria wasn't writing. The curator knit her brow. Her mouth bowed open as if to speak, but suddenly hesitant herself...until it clicked into place. "The initials you were just talking about."

"Could be a code, right? Like the Rendered and Rendered Unto God."

A nervous chuckle. "Tell me you got one more and I'm with you. Sort of."

Almost gleefully, Melody reached/squeezed Victoria's arm. Pulled back. Pulled the brake. Took a breath.

"I have more. It's the weirdest. But let's backpedal a little."

Melody pressed the heels of her palms on the table's edge. Created resistance with her arms as she squared her shoulders. Victoria liked the way she did that. And Melody spoke.

"Do you know the work my family is involved in?"

"Your father-in-law has a quiet kind of notoriety on Google."

"You probably know as much as I do. They are all in the same business. They don't share and I never ask. But I want to try it."

"Try it?"

"Try it out. Intelligence."

Victoria cocked a grin. "I think you're very smart."

"Very funny."

"I don't think I know what you mean."

"Like you said, look at this as a mystery. But I think a mystery—hunting clues to uncover a specific crime or culprit—is too narrow. I think this is bigger than that and different somehow. I think this is—and don't laugh at me—I'd like to go at this as though it's an intelligence operation."

Victoria didn't have an answer for that. Pinched an itch at the end of her nose. "Tell me what else you— Or why—?" Focused on Melody; didn't want to lose her. Clicked her pen. All business. "Tell me the other."

"Doris put a Post-it. A journal or diary page written by Turkey John Swan. It was the last thing I looked at. Did you see it?"

"I did."

"Talks about his daughter carving a message in the wharf posts. They're still there, the posts. All that re- mains of the wharf. But the words are still there, and they're readable. They were meant to last."

"They must be incredible artifacts."

"The twins—the whole family—call them their mer- maids."

"I'd love to see them."

"He calls it a 'challenge' and a 'parole.' I looked that up. It's called a recognition code. I am not making this up. Spies have used recognition codes since, well, the beginning of spying. For that sort of thing, it's common vernacular."

"Like a password."

Nods. "Like a password. To prove two strangers are safe with one another." Melody relaxed. Perfectly calm because she knew she was right. "The first one, the challenge is 'The Lord Giveth.' The 'parole' as Nika—that was the girl's name—as she changed it, it's 'The Water Show Us Forth.'"

Victoria paused her pen. "What did she change it from?"

"The Water Showeth Forth."

"From a general statement to a personal declaration."

"It's what the captured slaves cried in terror when they were delivered to Foxtail Farm and dragged into the torture chamber."

"The 'Inward Light, Place of Blackness.'"

Eyes flashing fire, Melody bobbed her head encouraging Victoria. Eyes focusing, as if seeing light through mist, Victoria matched Melody's affirmation with a gradual nod of her own. She said, "None ever seen again. Those words are in every account I've read."

For Melody, it was as if those lost voices spoke that very moment directly to her. Possessed with calm, her voice went soft. Low and from her gut. "Victoria, those wharf pilings have always been underwater. Turkey John verifies that in the page Doris put aside. Nika—his daughter—dives down, beneath the surface, to change the words. They were secret."

Discovery always played excitement for Melody. Burst from her; the explosion of sunlight hitting snow after a heavy fall. With Victoria, discovery settled inside her; overtook her as that moment when, hit by sunlight, snow changes to its liquid essence: clear water collapsed, spread and level.

"How did those slaves know—"

"That's what I'm saying!"

"—to give the parole? More importantly: why were they giving it?"

The charge of happiness burning inside Melody reminded her how sad she'd become. She quickly promised herself to be better. A better mother. A better wife. Better to her chosen family and better armed against Boone Kelso.

Victoria made notes and Melody waited. She watched as Victoria found the Doris/Turkey John Swan/Nika page of foolscap. Transcribed from it. Transcribed from documents Melody recognized from her reading of the horrors found in The Place of Blackness. And then she looked up. Cool and clear.

"What brought you here, Melody? Not today, specifically, but why this? Why now?"

You don't lie to your friend.

Melody's silence seemed to confirm something for Victoria. "You're not here to solve a mystery."

"Honestly, I appreciate your willingness to dig in and help me."

"You said you're gathering intelligence."

"I want the broadest, most accurate picture of my family's history of slavery I can assemble. I'm desperate for it."

"Intelligence is gathered—isn't it, usually?—to understand an enemy. To use it against them?"

"I'm trying to protect my father."

Silas: I choose you.

Melody must have been showing more emotion than she wanted, for Victoria reached across the table. Placed comforting fingers over Melody's nervous hands.

"I just want to understand. Protect from what?"

You trust your friend.

"My past."

"You don't want to tell me?"

"I want you to trust me."

Victoria removed her fingers. Clicked her pen. Closed her notebook. "Friends trust."

"Thanks."

They considered each other. Melody's sunlight reflected off of Victoria, the ripples that stirred her surface. They smiled at each other and sealed their friendship.

"Now's probably a good time to break. I have to pick up my twins."

"You'll come back?"

Melody agreed—after Thanksgiving—and Victoria opened one of the boxes. Removed a file she had prepared the day after Halloween. They would start, she said, with the counterfeit scalp and the death of Turkey John Swan's most peculiar victim, a slave named Cupid Scrapefoot Williams.

2.

Gary Gravin, Deputy Director for Operations, stalked to Lynn's desk. Pulled the bottom drawer. His gaze went from inside it to Lynn still at the door, rarely used anymore, that connected her office to his outer suite.

"Are you looking to wet your whistle or blow a police one?"

"One what?" He was a picture of disappointment. Regret.

"Whistle. Either way it doesn't feel very good."

"It's empty."

"Easy. I told you I quit."

"I'm sorry I looked."

"You're not. Just searching for an easy way to gather your courage." Lynn pointed at her white sofa. "We can have this talk like the friends we've always been, side by side, or you can take one of these." She placed a hand on the white leather edge of a straight back accent chair.

"You take the sofa." He took the chair. Waited for her to cross her legs. Face him. "You know how concerned I've been. Since Michael."

A tight fake smile in answer.

"Since Michael's disappearance— Lynn, you've been completely out of control."

"You've done zero to help."

"That's not fair. Anyway, I'm told Michael is contained."

"That's bullshit and you don't even know what it means. I took a pair of scissors to my throat."

"Your recklessness, your unhealthy desire to push at something you've no business pushing at—you are restricted and were ordered away from—"

"KALEIDOSCOPE."

"—put you in harm's way."

Tapped the small weal at the center of her jugular notch. "This is my fault?"

"It bought you a reprieve. I thought your transfer to Foreign Resources would help you succeed. I thought, with some success, which you were showing, this door between us might have gone back to a functioning part of our work together."

"Like prison rehabilitates."

"Your Division Manager—"

"Sexy Steph' the Bitch Boss?"

"God dammit! Stop fucking around, Lynn! She's put in a recommendation for your termination! It has teeth. I don't see it not proceeding."

♛ ♛ ♛

NATIONAL RESOURCES/FOREIGN RESOURCES Division Manager Stephanie Malkinson meets with Lynn inside her office in the green glass goblin of the New Headquarters

Building. Not as large or as comfortably appointed as Lynn's office in the Old Headquarters Building. Gray and murkily lit, oddly L-shaped, it displays a messy pair of bookshelves— "displayed" because their messiness reads purposeful. Disorganized books and memo print-outs and folders obviously not important/valuable because they aren't locked up anywhere, share space with trinkets and souvenirs from countries and operations Stephanie Malkinson never operated in or on, like a collection of scalps belonging to everyone else but her. Her desk sports a family reunion of photos—Lynn peers over the tops, before taking her chair, the frame backs: a blank and meager breastwork between her and her boss.

Stephanie sits formally in an over-engineered ergonomic, possibly multi-level (possibly dental), office chair behind her protective 4x6, 5x5, 5x7, 8x10 crenellations. Behind her, hung like warrior shields but not: brassy mundane plaques, and glossy photographs: Stephanie making nice with both Bushes; Stephanie and two former Agency directors. "Tough Stephanie" catches a marlin, her smile sharp and as slick as the fish's sword. Tucked on the side wall—but Lynn has noticed—a group photo. Grins, smiles, giggles, and laughs. Senate floor. Stephanie rubbing shoulders with Gary's wife. Senator Theresa Ossani, Chair of the Senate Select Committee.

The whole office reeks of stale bread that knows where/begs for the butter she's all for getting smeared with.

"I want to find common ground, Lynn. Before we went wrong of each other."

"Before me met?"

"Okay. Yes." Stephanie makes her eyes big. Widen past the wires of her John Lennon/Manhattan loft psychiatrist glasses. "We can agree we received the same basic training at The Farm."

Lynn inclines her head. Taps one of Stephanie's desk photos. Subtly, but not too subtly, she moves it. Bangalores an open path between them. "Handsome family. You must make them proud."

Stephanie—subtly/not subtly—shifts it back. "What is the number one method for recruitment of a successful agent?"

"Patriotic/ideologic zeal cross-purpose to their nation's current leadership, policies, positions, laws, etcetera that pale next to the beacon of freedom represented by the U-S-of-A."

Lynn received a blank look of intentional incomprehension from her division manager. "Your level of sarcasm borders on outright insubordination, which your behavior has already demonstrated is your cheap stock in trade. I want a serious answer. Now."

Lynn moistened her lips; a lot to say on the subject, she didn't want them chapped before she finished. "By 'successful,' do you mean depth of commitment, trust, longevity, level of risk they're willing to take, ability to push them beyond that level?"

"Yes, I—"

"Wait. And when they want to give up. Quit. An ability to force them to continue under you. Put forth that extra umpf?"

"Aptly put. All of those."

Lynn let the pendulum swing a tick-tock or two before she lowered it to slice.

"Sex."

Stephanie Malkinson didn't flinch. "Greed. As in money is number one. Greed is what they teach. That's what we're supposed to learn. Sexual relations between an officer and an asset or agent: we have a strict policy to refrain from in all circumstances."

"Of course we entrap foreign targets, we induce recruitments, reward agents and assets all the time, everywhere with sex."

"The use of sex workers, honeytraps—I'm not arguing that. We *don't personally engage in sexual relations—as you have done—in the recruitment or running of agents because it opens* us *to compromise.* And *emotional conflict which can be a dangerous/life-threatening, self-sabotaging form of entrapment."*

Tick-tock. Tick-tock. "Yeah. I don't suffer that virtuous a conscience. Intel agencies worldwide—sex is the most often employed, most successful inducement to long-term recruitment, trust, compromise, and commitment. Far more powerful than the old payola."

Lynn pretends she hasn't noticed the color leaving Stephanie's face. But it started in her throat and has reached the worry lines dropping from her crinkled brow.

"Have you always held this wrong-think attitude?"

Lynn moves the photograph, aggressively this time.

"Would answer the question why I've spent my career behind a desk."

Hand like a snake-strike, Stephanie slaps the frame face down and thrusts a fang-finger through the opening aimed at Lynn's throat. "You are too protected for me to recommend what you richly deserve. Termi-

nation. Without prejudice. I am recommending—urging/demanding—your reassignment out of my division."
Jerky. Manic. Waves paperwork. "Until such a time, this division will have you on administrative leave—"

"Paid?"

"Shut your damn mouth. You will break off all contact with Roman Sayadov, Elmin Hasanov, any other contacts you've made with Azerbaijani embassy personnel, including your gay, car-dealing, tennis-playing partner—"

"What are you bringing up his sexual preference for? You know, we have rules about that kind of bigoted, anti—"

"You're a fucking train wreck. Take this—"

She shoves Lynn's copy of her reprimand and leave order into Lynn's waiting hand. "Get out of here."

Lynn backs away. The corner of the L. "Sorry we never really hit it off. I would just say this—about money?"

Stephanie Malkinson straightens her desk.

"Anyone can be trained to offer it. Pay it. Anyone can pass it. But it's a thing. Picked up. Put down. Always space to change your mind between. The other?"

Lynn barely disguised her smile to see her former boss looking. Engaged. Waiting.

"The other you gotta be good at. All in, with your warm body and your cold, dead heart. All in all the way, and that's why it works better and longer and is more efficiently cruel and mentally binding and imprisoning to a case officer's will than money."

❦ ❦ ❦

"Termination? Thought it was administrative leave before reassignment."

"Your last little speech put her over the top." Pained. "Why'd you do it?"

"Screw him?"

"Have sex with a potential agent. Yes."

"To make him not 'potential.' And I'm still doing it."

"I'm going to pretend you didn't just say that."

"Because it hurts you personally? We never had anything, Gary. You're married."

He came to his feet. Towered over her. On purpose menace. Posture nailing exactly what she's intimated.

"We're finished, Lynn."

Lynn shrugged. Zero emotion. Brushed past him. Shoulder against his arm. On purpose, too. Went to her desk. Front side. "You and Ms. Malkinson miss the point." Her purse. Reaches in. "I'll pack my desk, sign whatever you want. Won't cry to Daddy."

"Lynn." Total misinterpretation. He's two steps behind her back. Not touching her shoulders but looking. "Lynn."

She turned, aware of where he stood, so much so that her hand matched his. She tucked a folded sheet of yellow pad paper between his thumb and forefinger. Eyes locked the whole time with him. Waited. Gary stepped back. Unfolded it.

A sloppy ink sketch. Diagram of something. Numbers. Azeri letters. Electronic notations scribbled.

"What's this?"

Clear-eyed and unassailable. "Bios chipset. Copied from a manual. Those are the hardware switches. It's the Azeri proprietary version of the Gretacoder 605."

"A cipher machine."

"The model of data encryptor in the Azerbaijan embassy dedicated to Russian traffic. The operator is rotating back to Baku, and Roman—"

"Your code clerk."

"Is moving up. Or hopes to. He's training on it."

"And how did you see the manual?"

She cocked her head. Smug. Smirk. "Used something better than money. When bachelors are sloppy and pussy-whipped, they're dopey."

Gary found a seat. Took her debrief. Kept the paper drawing. It changed everything.

"You serious you can keep this going with this target without getting into an emotional fuck-up?"

"Uh-huh."

"Did you have this?" He fluttered the yellow paper. "When you met with her?"

"Uh-huh. Do you think my termination is going to go through or are you going to get Stephanie Malkinson off my back?"

"Bitch boss?"

Big grin.

"You're a piece of work, Lynn."

"This whole time, you haven't come after me on the sex of it all."

"I don't want to think of you that way. I think too much of you."

"In that way."

"I think too much of you, Lynn."

Lynn watched the door close behind him. Listened for the click. One-two-three. She reached for her wrist. Popped the clasp on her large silver bangle. Took a full-mouth hit of gin from the disguised flask. Fire flash. Felt it. Visualized it. Hated herself that much more for it.

LYNN KINGSTON DRANK her flask, four ounces, empty. Knew she wouldn't, and didn't, get anywhere near the place she wanted. Needed. Four months sober, she'd have thought, would have bought her a little less tolerance.

Plenty more at home. My Kingsbury home, and my other I haven't seen in a month.

Since coming on strong with Roman on Halloween, and a day later—situating herself in her Layla Kingsbury cover which only warranted wardrobe and makeup, the two things OTS couldn't fabricate for the lived-in parallel life they created, her "new-to-Lynn/been-there-three-years-Layla Rock Creek townhouse—"

Have to admit: step up from my place.

Started showing up at "her"/Layla's H&R Block franchise office. Ducked in "hellos" to her retail neighbors. One way or the other shrugs from most staffs, but a gratifying "Hiya Layla's" from three of the seven strip mall business owners. Started learning the software. Reading accounting manuals, learning her day job cover. Desirous to weigh Roman's official interest, his security apparatus' engagement, she added peculiarity to her drive to work. One that—with one-way streets, an unavoidable U-turn, a necessary one-street over-shoot/backtrack, to place her correct side of the street at an eventual stop before an upscale townhouse. A curb/car-sit for a few minutes, drinking coffee, gazing at the townhouse's dark and uncommunicative façade.

Puzzle piece bait for putting together the Layla Kingsbury secret.

Don't want the cat to scratch the upholstery, set up a cat-scratcher.

When they dig at your past, aiming to friend-or-foe you, best thing—and always done—give them a secret to uncover all on their own. Something that makes you real, gives them a sense of accomplishment, and paints you, ultimately, more sympathetic than neutral.

A tumor that starts out scary, turns out benign.

Sip. Watch the strange, dark townhouse; sip, watch a left-on porch light—coachman fixture missing its crown, glass panels cracked—flicker dim hint of doleful vacancy.

Maybe picked up a tail once, maybe just coincidence. Never a reappearing vehicle, never one behind or ahead ever slowed/sped up/showed interest in her final approach and turn into the retail mall/H&R Block parking lot.

Saturday, three days after their Old Carriage House fuckfest, Lynn accepted a tennis invite. Same crew—Aydin, nail-salon Cathy, and this time Layla partnered with Roman—and they shared the rest of the day. Bought her an expensive, lingering lunch. Afternoon and night, his apartment. Now, halfway into November, and to every-one's anger—

My own, if I had the guts or the shame to admit it

—she spent three nights a week in Roman's bed; woke him up, her hand wagging—

"Roman, you got kids you're not telling me about?"

"No." Shy/embarrassed. Shit—really, goofy/sweet.

—a funny T-Rex dinosaur alarm clock going off like a stepped-on-tail cat more than any King of the Thunder Lizards.

"I just always had it in my bedroom. I packed it when I deployed."

That and the shelf of Funko Pop! big head Marvel figures his mom loved giving him for birthdays and holidays.

"Would have broke her heart if I'd left those behind." With a good-natured chuckle.

Childlike and wrapped up in a game that wasn't for kids; lackadaisical with the grown-up rules. How she got her look at the Gretacoder manual. Out for a jog. The Rock Creek Trail that winds along the stream. She steered the breathy conversation to movies. Admitted she hadn't seen *The Avengers.* Whatdy'ya know? His all-time fave. Layla, sorry she missed it.

"You haven't. Biggest blockbuster of the year—it's not going anywhere. Hold on, let me check."

Out with the phone. Local multiplex: timing worked; tickets booked. "Just need a quick rinse and we got this."

Back at his place. Invite to join in. "Honey, I do that, we aren't going to make that show."

"Alright, alright."

Roman into the shower. Lynn into Roman's briefcase. The cipher machine manual should never have left the embassy; the Layla Kingsbury's of the world, the exact reason why.

Lynn hated superhero CGI crap, but Layla loved it, gushingly so. Superheroes became their thing; he caught her up on Marvel and DC, and alcohol helped with that. But later, *The Avengers* night, snuggled aglow in his bed, she told him how great his cousin Aydin was; she was taking delivery on the Mercedes SLS the next morning. "Not Tony Stark's Acura NSX, but it'll do."

He laughed. His job didn't allow flash, but he shared how he hoped soon to upgrade his BMW— "Just need to ace my promotion. The studying involved is driving me nuts."

"I'm happy to help."

"And I wish you could, but this stuff..." He sliced the air with his hand, made a show of tightening his lips. Signal: cut off/can't talk about that.

Of course, like catnip, *that* was all that Gary and B-Boss Stephanie wanted. Happy for Lynn to do whatever it took to get access. Inside. Flash that BIOs. Burn a trojan horse into the hardware.

Mid-November, question for Lynn became what compartment of Roman's personality would get her there. She knew his two public sides: the playful side that enjoyed CGI movies, enjoyed sports and fitness, bar-hopping to see where/what the night brought you; neon, jukebox, pool table/darts, door curtained by cigarette smoke, or dim light cocktail nightclub corners. Slick hair good stories/good laughs. Slick dance floor denizens. Dreamy sparkle, and car-washed-curbside looking good. Where smoking happened in the cigar room. The other side was dinner and genuine conversation. About the city. About ambitions. The culture of things and the news of the day. The world. Out to dinner with Roman was to go out with a gentleman who knew that you achieve your dreams, not by imposing them on your space, but find where in the space you move through, the space you share, they reveal themselves their best. To their best. No fear and know when to laugh. When to place your bet.

If Layla Kingsbury were smart, she'd hold on to that man and make sure she didn't lose him. Lynn Kingston needed to hold on just as hard, find that blind spot between maturity and youth. Where she could fool one side into betraying the other. Roman into betraying his country. He'd either volunteer his services—get the access CIA required—or, more than likely, Lynn would have to compromise him. Heart/soul/career. They'd hold him in place running the tap on the Russian-dedicated cipher machine indefinitely, if they could, or the Agency would parachute him out and he'd switch places with "Layla". Never see her again. He'd take her place living a false life—

Some random town no one knows

No one wants to find or visit

Wrung out and ruined like a dirty rag thrown away by me.

It was lunchtime. She'd take it late from the sack at her Office Depot desk at her strip mall office, call Roman and step it up. Plan a dinner-date, a back-to-his-place, a let's-not-do-it/let's-talk-about-us (this-probably-won't-work out), "okay-let's-I-want-you-so-bad."

She knew the empty space between the two sides of his personality she'd attack. The one thing he never brought up. A hovering ghost between them. It disgusted Lynn that she knew exactly what they meant. The bobblehead toys his mom "forced" him to take and the way he whispered in her ear when at their closest, asked her to say "daddy" at the highest height before collapse.

And, without enough gin, God damn, but it all looks so ugly this side of lunch.

3.

T HE OTHER SIDE OF the building. Same side of lunch. Director's Executive Dining Room. Silas, Harker, a waiter. One of a trio of staff—waiter, chef, bus boy/dishwasher who hold security clearance as high as some members of Congress, while making far less in tips. Where Director Jeremy Harker III would remember this day as the first day of the end of KALEIDOSCOPE, Silas would remember it as "the idiot with the soup" day.

"What is your soup of the day?" Silas didn't like the chowder option on the menu.

The gleam-faced waiter dropped his adverb and any sense of the justice that lives in all forms of the word *just*, and said, "So you know, sir—we proudly prepare and serve our cream of broccoli lactose-free."

"Lactose-free. But I may presume it's still dairy based?"

"Oh, no, sir. It's dairy-free as well."

"How creamy."

The waiter helped himself to a smile. "Our second soup of the day, the butternut squash soup, contains both butter and cream cheese."

"No milk?"

"Almond milk, sir."

"Such small nipples. I'll have a cup of the chili con carne."

"Shrimp cocktail for me." Director Harker ordered with a game wink at Silas, "but only if they lack toes and fingers."

"We serve them peeled, sir."

Harker gave a dead-eye. Peeled off. To Silas: "How many of these luncheons have we had?"

"'Luncheons.' First was in July when you invited me back to the Agency—"

"You invited yourself back, Silas."

"I invited you into KALEIDOSCOPE's current operations."

"We'll get to that. But, once a month, since July, you and I have broken bread in my dining room."

An intimate reception room opened into 292 square feet of dining area meticulously appointed with the CIA seal subtly stamped, embossed, emblazoned so that no matter where you look you are bound to understand you are being looked metaphorically and quietly overwhelmingly looked back at in china, crystal, silver, and fabric. Room for up to ten guests. Only the appropriate table would ever be inside the room at any time. Today, situated in the room's center stood a round table that, larger than a two-top would never seat more than three people comfortably. Built, secured, and opened in 2005—four years after Harker's initial Agency career—this was better by far than the buffet he'd brought into the DCI's conference room during his epic (and losing) battles against Nathan Muir alive and dead.

Silas made an issue of polishing a water spot from his empty wineglass. "With this being our second lunch in

November. May I assume today is our own little Thanksgiving?"

"You've not been thankful."

"To you?"

"Yes, Silas. To me."

"Personally?"

"I think that's obvious."

"Far be it from me to correct you on something so nebulous as your personal interpretation of the meaning of a holiday. Jeremy, from my perspective, you have Thanksgiving all wrong."

"This isn't about Thanksgiving. I have reached the limits of my patience with you. More than that—a heck of a lot more—I have been forthcoming with the intelligence you've requested. You've not been forthcoming with anything KALEIDOSCOPE is doing, has done, plans to do in the future. That ends today."

"You're right, Jeremy. You have been generous. Extremely so. Are you ready?"

"I've made myself clear."

"Thank you and Happy Thanksgiving."

"That's not how this works. Not with me at the helm. No, sir."

He'd made it to Acting Director a decade ago; ousted by Silas Kingston but now, returned, he saw himself as something of a Cincinnatus back from the plow. Before his resignation over the unfortunate experience of Operation ATROPOS, his exemplary career only had three hiccups. Nathan Muir, Tom Bishop, Russell Aiken: dead/presumed dead/retired. To Harker's credit, the legend of fierce determination for the ops and operators he ran, and for his Seventh Floor fancy footwork as

DDO that simultaneously rid the Agency of Cold War deadwood preparing the way for the www-dot-twenty-first-century new world order while simultaneously, having missed, entirely, zero blame/responsibility/blowback from 9/11 and the subsequent War on Terror. His wins were far greater than his losses. ATROPOS had prevented a nuclear device delivered into Al-Qaeda's hand, May 2001. Prior to that, right hand to CIA legend Gus Avrokotos, he oversaw the delivery/disbursement of Congressman Charlie Wilson and CIA legend/Pentagon embed Gus Avrokotos weapons to the Mujahideen resistance in the Soviet-Afghan War. When Avrokotos moved to Central America ops, Jeremy Harker danced out of the way of the Iran-Contra boobytrap Avrokotos blew the whistle on before getting whistled out for his troubles. '98-'99, an expert at moving arms, Harker distinguished himself setting up the Kosovo weapons pipeline that financed the KLA guerrilla army against Serbia; the Albanian "hunting clubs" that skirted US federal law and delivered armor-piercing Barrett rifles, while hedging the Agency's bets with Croatia—modernizing their military through CIA front operation Military Professional Resources Inc. and Bosnia through a similar company, DynCorp.

"Do you honestly think you're above the law?"

It was that. Exactly that. With all his history and without a spark of irony. Silas despised Harker. That Harker didn't know more than believe the words coming out his mouth. It set Silas's teeth.

"No more than this Agency."

"The CIA is bound by law."

"Please, Jeremy. We could turn this place upside down. Give it a few shakes, see what falls out of its pockets, and—"

"Everything would be legal."

"Everything the CIA does, top to bottom, is legal?"

"Absolutely—"

Chili served. Shrimp served. Qualifier served—

"Within the framework of this government."

"What you're trying to say is that you have constitutional, congressional, judicial, executive exemptions from choice civil and federal and international laws."

"You know what I mean."

"Then you'll understand this. KALEIDOSCOPE has legal exemptions and superseding mandates that are beyond yours."

Silas crushed his saltines inside their plastic wrapper. "Amazing. Spent my entire life taking them out and pinching them into my bowl. My daughter-in-law taught me this trick."

"Silas, I don't want this to go where I am prepared to take it."

"Toot-toot. You're driving the train."

"But everywhere I look, or attempt to look, I am locked out of KALEIDOSCOPE. This administration vowed to the American people that we would have a sweeping series of transparency reforms."

"I recall. 'My Administration is committed to creating an unprecedented level of openness in Government.' Big fan of that. Got my vote." Silas enjoyed a bit of chili. "Should have asked for chili in the first place, but was afraid it would be vegan." He watched the blood beat in the zigzag vein on the side of the director's face. "You think the president meant KALEIDOSCOPE. Have you asked him?"

"I don't answer to you. You answer to me."

"Okay. You did. Let me guess. President Obama told you to ask your boss and mine—as far as sharing intelligence goes—the DNI and they told you...?"

Zigzag, zigzag, zigzag.

"To ask me. Ol' Silas Kingston, who never did no one no wrong."

"You make this extremely easy for me. I'm not asking. I'm telling. You give me everything you're running, or it is over."

"Jeremy, you know everything I'm running. The Baku situation—you've approved every piece of intelligence I've requested. And Operation KASHASP at Camp Abu Omar."

"Keep dissembling. This doesn't end well. You opened the door for me, and I don't like what I see—"

"Because I left the screen door locked."

"The days of a KALEIDOSCOPE adjacent/restricted/oversight/approval-required stamp and redactions are ending."

"You keep saying that. Look, Jeremy—"

"I prefer you address me as 'Director.'"

"Director: you're not the first Director to feel this way. To want precisely the same thing."

"Which one?"

"The ninth one. Apparently, he felt the same way you do, had the same questions. Was director for exactly five months."

"You're full of shit. That's not what happened with James Schlesinger."

"Interesting you say that. In 1975, when Senator Church led his investigation into CIA abuses, which gave up the Crown Jewels, all our dirtiest secrets, and almost destroyed the Agency, Mr. Church came to your same conclusion vis-à-vis Schlesinger and KALEIDO-SCOPE."

"There is zero mention of KALEIDOSCOPE in the Church Committee Report."

"I often wonder why that is. He certainly was thorough in dismantling so much of what went on here. And yet, KALEIDOSCOPE never came up. James Angleton, my mentor—also before your time, but he'd have liked you—forced to resign Christmas Eve, 1974, right before the shit hit the fan, that man, afterward, would say, when I visited him in Tucson, 'Silas, it was as if that Senator Church had inside help.'"

The spotless waiter delivered entrees. A cilantro lime cream sauce over grilled chicken breast for Silas. Fish for Harker. First time since July, Rainbow Trout was on the menu. Silas watched as Harker prepared his utensils like a surgeon, preparation for removal of—

"Where's the head?"

"Sir, we removed it and the bones for you. The chef remembered you'd made that request—to always removed the head—after we'd served it last time." A not-so-subtle eye shift at Silas to remind the director.

"Does take some dexterous knife work. I remember it being marvelous," Silas said.

Harker gestured it served.

"Lactose free, too." Silas showed his teeth at the waiter's face. When the man left, he resumed. "I'll take the opportunity here—Director Harker—to help you understand KALEIDOSCOPE. From my point of view."

"About time. Go on." Nibbled. Didn't like fish. Ever.

"CIA acts as firefighters."

"We put out fires. In most cases, before they happen."

"Here's the thing. Whether you're working from immediate intelligence or an intelligence profile many years in the collection, you're acting or reacting on immediate situations—firefighters—and, let's both admit, sometimes arsonists."

"I know what we do. I thought you were going to background me on what you do."

"In 1948, the Haifa pipeline ran from Kirkuk— Iraq into Israel."

"Yes. Cancelled by Iraq when Israel became a nation."

"Except as part of Operation KALEIDOSCOPE, it wasn't. KALEIDOSCOPE kept it running and Iraq profited. Israel profited. That's why the Middle East, vis-à-vis Israel, all the chances thrown that way, never blew up into World War Three. See, when things looked to get out of hand, KALEIDOSCOPE was there at the spigot. The flow of oil provided peaceful leverage until Saddam Hussein took over Iraq in 1979. He immediately shut down the pipeline."

"Okay. If we're going to go one-by-one, we'll be here all day and get nowhere."

"That's the firefighter mentality. KALEIDOSCOPE is not a single operation, it's a series of integrated systems in constant give-and-take flux, like the turning of its namesake, until all reach equilibrium and the patterns form a perfect picture."

"Give and take with whom?"

"Kalaydoskop—"

"That is?"

"Once Soviet, now Russian. Mirror-operation, runs parallel, turns its lens in opposition."

"Never heard of it."

"And 'you're welcome.' After Saddam shut it down—the Kirkuk Pipeline—it became easy for Kalaydoskop to destroy portions of that pipeline and make it inoperable for the future. At the same time—1979—Kalaydoskop went on the offense against KALEIDOSCOPE here at home. Ran a dis-info campaign in America to create a gas crisis at the pumps. Reality was that under Nixon, prices were higher and supply lower. Conspiracy theorists claim alternately that Carter wanted to go green, that his administration artificially created the crisis; other theory—Exxon, Chevron, you-name-it Big Oil, artificially inflated prices."

"That *is* what happened."

"It isn't. The Kalaydoskop preferred Ronald Reagan over Jimmy Carter—"

"Oh, come on!"

"Carter's foreign policy emphasized winning the Cold War through human rights campaigns."

"And Reagan, the threat of nuclear war. Guess who won?" Harker made another stab at his fish.

"The nuke threat—dealt with effectively since World War Two, was not as frightening to the Soviets as a popular uprising. Never has been, never will be."

"Ridiculous."

"Really? Did I miss a war? Because I saw the people in Poland, in Romania in the streets and squares; in

Germany with their little hammers all along the Wall. Weren't no bombs going off."

"Get back to KALEIDOSCOPE."

"In retaliation—the Kirkuk pipeline, the gas crisis—KALEIDOSCOPE made the Soviets believe they were going to lose their puppet government in Afghanistan. This would cut the Sovs off from gas they were stealing from that country after the Iranian Revolution cut their primary source. KALEIDOSCOPE played into their deeper fear of losing Afghanistan as the buffer to their interior. Neither of these was the case, but KALEIDOSCOPE wanted Kalaydoskop bogged down in a war.

"Jeremy—I'm sorry—Director: you get to set the menu in this dining room today because of the work you did against the Soviets in Afghanistan. Dismantling KALEIDOSCOPE would dismantle your greatest benefactor."

"Ahh. KALEIDOSCOPE: the hidden hand."

"No. CIA's the hidden hand. We're the glove sometimes pulled over it."

They ate for a moment, Silas still working on his chili, chicken going untouched. He explained how KALEIDOSCOPE was against the work Avrokotos/Harker did for the Mujahideen; where this, the weaponizing of future enemies the CIA is particularly good at—

"Now, I have to stop you. I wasn't here, but no one could have predicted 9/11 in 1988."

"No, and KALEIDOSCOPE was prevented from stopping you. And no one did predict it or get fired for missing it. I viewed it the same way I viewed Persia. We had it good there with the Shah and the oil situation—our primary/only objective—but the Agency kept growing the Shah's military control over the country, creating a situation ripe for revolution. Happened the same way back then, way before Al-Qaeda. No one predicted. No one to blame. No one to fire."

Silas got the bright waiter's attention. Asked for his entrée bagged to take home. And would the chef add a side of the cilantro lime cream sauce in a separate container?

Said, "The KALEIDOSCOPE theory is power and peace through energy control, not warfare. KALEIDO-SCOPE is against creating our own monsters we have to fight later. We take our pokes on the chin. Adjust the lens; keep trying to frame a balanced picture."

Silas continued into the 1980s. Iran/Iraq War. "CIA supports Saddam Hussein with weapons. Soviet Union: the same. Regionally, both KALEIDOSCOPE and Kalaydoskop aligned together against Iran."

"That's fairly outrageous to admit. If I'm following you. You've just now made the claim that a US intelligence operation conducted business with an enemy intel service. How deep did this cooperation go?"

"We rarely hide our moves from the enemy. Same way with them. Conceptualize it as chess."

"The spy game is all chess."

"Wrong. Chess is played with open moves between opponents."

"This isn't a game."

"You used the phrase. Since we're playing a single game for world hegemony, and both trying to avoid Armageddon, it's best neither side makes mistakes. Now, follow me. The upside for both Kaleidoscopes is to hurt

Iran through helping Saddam, trying to lead him to a more moderate position toward us. Meanwhile, KALEIDOSCOPE goes all in with the Royal Family of Kuwait. We get them to support Iraq and thereby put Iraq in debt to Kuwait and leverage stability after war when, we believe, our support of Saddam Hussein will see him come out more moderate *to us*."

The waiter delivered the box. Silas ignored him. He put it beside his elbow.

"The Soviet Union collapses."

"KALEIDSCOPE want to take credit for that? Am I going to hear that next?" Exasperated with his fish, Harker pushed the plate away.

"Iran is weak, but radical Islam is strong. Not only in Iran, who, depleted in overt military power from the war, now go one hundred and ten percent supporting proxy radical Islam. Iran sees that arming and stoking radicals is their only way to maintain power. KALEIDOSCOPE also has a bigger problem. CIA armed those radicals in Afghanistan who are now looking for new enemies—the result of which, we've discussed.

"Kalaydoskop tells Saddam Hussein that the US is untrustworthy. To prove it, they expose to Saddam Hussein that CIA—not KALEIDOSCOPE—was using the Contras to get weapons to Iran. Russia convinces Saddam to invade Kuwait, who they insist is an American/KALEIDOSCOPE puppet. Another CIA rake-stepping war. Saddam invades Kuwait, which is a win for Kalaydoskop and opposite of what KALEIDOSCOPE wanted. But in for a penny, in for a pound. Best end result? Go all the way and take out Saddam Hussein and partition Iraq. Bush/Cheney, however, chicken out.

"Kalaydoskop helps Yeltsin, easy to manipulate, into power. Convince him that the Middle East is quicksand to bury Russia; to let the US get buried there. Turn their attention to *exporting* gas. Now, KALEIDOSCOPE is on defense as Russia is negotiating pipelines *into* Turkey. *Into* Syria. Kalaydoskop is slowly building toward being the number one gas exporter in the world... Their eye on the prize of securing Europe *not through war* but through energy. This jumps us up to this year's Baku Oil Conference, which I went out of my way to include you in."

"Wiretaps, surveillance, industrial espionage—if I understand you, the highest order of your business and entirely against our charter."

"But 9/11 brought us the Iraq War. Our defining dream for KALEIDOSCOPE is on the ropes. What the Bush/Cheney crowd came to understand—passed down to the new guy, and everyone who counts in Congress—is that war is extraordinarily profitable. Not just the military industrial complex component—and that's big bucks all-time, everywhere since Eisenhower's warning—but even more wealth to be had in post-conflict infrastructure reconstruction. War is good for profit and profit is good for power. And while our war in Iraq tied the US down, Kalaydoskop captured Northern Europe with energy, not war at all."

"Believe me, Europe is just fine."

"Until the hand on Nord Stream One decides to turn it off."

"Nord Stream *One*?"

"Two's coming. That's what we must and will counter at Baku. KALEIDOSCOPE is going to broker the alternative to Russian power that will deliver more energy faster, cheaper, cleaner, and plentifully than Kalaydoskop."

Silas finished. He folded his napkin. Took his to-go into his lap. Harker could only stare, annoyed incredulity coupled with an icy terror of total belief. Silas struck the nail into the coffin. "Here's the thing. And you will not like it. We don't work toward the same goal. In fact, KALEIDOSCOPE tried and failed to prevent the creation of the CIA. It was felt that the brand of intelligence you centralize here is, ultimately, about military might and fighting wars."

"Of course, *winning* wars, but more importantly, preventing them."

"You haven't done a very good job of that."

"Next, you'll tell me, you have?"

"No. Otherwise the job we set out to do after the First World War would have been completed and the ordinal determiner 'First' would have been an unnecessary eventuality."

"The magical, mystical KALEIDOSCOPE, saving the world."

"I used to think so. Not sure you, or I, or our enemies can do that anymore. I'll ask you this. Hypothetically. If we could. If we could put you and war out of business, brought you that offer on a silver platter through total dominance/acquiescence of energy control, coupled with a big fat international buyout—"

"Buyout from what?"

"War/war-making, the ability/desire to wage it. The energy sector makes more money than the military industrial complex."

"Hypothetically, this sounds like communism or socialism."

"Which is why the Marxism/Leninism/communism/socialism quartet-*ism* is our biggest competitor. Taking individual greed out of the equation, central control comes about when those in power believe the people they govern, if left to their own devices, are stupid and spiteful; whose aim in life—left to their own petty devices—is the worst of human instinct. We believe if given freedom, humanity aims life at the bullseye of goodness and justice. But back to my question. Were that offer available, would humanity, the citizens of the world, take it?"

"Hypothetically. Strictly. Yes."

"In reality?"

"That kind of money doesn't exist. I think you're full of shit. Maybe even crazy. I think I will unravel KALEIDOSCOPE, have it dismantled, and, if warranted, have you and your network charged with crimes which may go as far as treason."

Silas pushed back his chair. Stood over the table.

"You've entirely missed my point. KALEIDOSCOPE is an empty folder."

"Excuse my Latin sloganeering, but fuck you."

"Jeremy, this is one of the few moments in my life I'm being honest. KALEIDOSCOPE is an empty folder into which anything can be dropped, making that thing larger, more dangerous, and, therefore, more terrifying to our opponent. It operates the most powerful weapon of the twentieth century that made its way into the twenty-first and shows no sign of being overtaken."

"What weapon is that?"

"The thing on which every fortune has risen, and every fallen nation has been razed. Marketing." Silas gave his bag a shake. "Thanks for lunch."

Harker scooted back. Didn't get up. Hung himself in his chair—elbows jutting from the arms, legs wide. Looked as stupid as Pacino did in some movie Harker appeared to be modelling.

"It's a holiday weekend, Silas. By December first, I'll have your 'marketing' plan. This will include an inventory— 'shopping list' if that helps your imagination—of founding documents, orders, charter, mandates, correspondences. List it and be thorough. Anything not listed we discover later—and we will—will be considered obstruction, withholding evidence, etcetera-etcetera and carry the appropriate USC Title 18 criminal charges. Along with that submission will be a road map of all operations undertaken by KALEIDOSCOPE during your authority and, prior to your ascension to its 'directorship'—" a scoffing chortle— "The names of all former directors and their operations to the level of your awareness. Last, regarding your two operations—as they are ongoing and I assume, have personnel in the field, you will begin coordinating immediately with DDO Gravin their return of control to Operations. KALEIDOSCOPE will go under review December first—"

"That's a Saturday."

"I don't fucking care. Our review will carry on to December twenty-first—a Friday—with a final determination, Monday thirty-one December."

"2013 would be the first year since 1919 that will begin without KALEIDOSCOPE."

"Yes, Mr. Kingston, that is my intention. It's all in this letter." He took a sealed envelope from his inside breast pocket. Made Silas reach for it. "You've become a victim of your own eventualities."

Silas snatched the crisp white envelope. "Eventualities don't happen to KALEIDOSCOPE. We are the eventuality."

FIRST GAS STATION out the Dolley Madison gate, Silas pulled his Cadillac to the center column between the pumps of the center island. Visually obscured from street and store, from the building's security camera.

"What is your soup of the day?" Sign.

"We proudly prepare and serve our cream of broccoli lactose-free." Countersign.

Dumped the lousy chicken into the garbage bin.

"Lactose-free. But I may presume it's still dairy based?" All clear.

"Oh, no, sir. It's dairy-free as well." Confirmation.

"How creamy." Proceed.

Retrieved the radio crystals hidden inside the side container of sauce.

Saturday, November Seventeenth

1.

SURVEILLANCE OF LAYLA KINGSBURY began when Lynn left the Rock Creek townhouse for tennis. Out the gate, front and follow cars. Quick decision: make half her morning run; stop by the vacant townhouse, dangle the bait. Debated popping into her H&R office but, on assumption they might have a team jonesing to go inside, she let the box shift around her—two new vehicles ahead/behind, the others out of sight now, somewhere on her three and nine flanks—and rolled away from the mystery house, headed for the tennis club.

Roman waiting. Quick romantic kiss, she returned with equal vigor. Found a doubles pair on the board. Won. Then to the juice bar and the lousy concoctions they whipped up from berries people used to never eat nor combine with grass goats would turn their noses up to.

They cheers'd. Roman: "To whisky." Layla/Lynn: "Gin." Roman: "The weekend?" Layla/Lynn: "We have any plans?" Eyes peering up from her straw. "Outdoor or indoor?" Roman: "If you let me drive your beast, I do have something... What if I said, grab an overnight bag?" Layla/Lynn: "I'd say, let's go."

Elmin and Aydin had planned an escape to a fancy manor-slash-farm-slash-boutique B and B, but duty called and Elmin was being "held captive" at the embassy. "They offered it to us," and he had his kit already/all ready in his gym bag.

Lynn slapped her keys in his palm. "'Drive, she said.'"

"'Just drive.' Stan Ridgeway." He led them to her SLS.

"*The Big Heat*. Great album."

"Eighties forever." And they laughed.

Back to the townhouse. A Charter Cable van at the end of her lane. Three-man team; one prepping to go up the pole for overwatch, the other two, Lynn assumed, would door-to-door once she left, get a read on the neighbors before entering her place.

He pulled in front of her door.

"Keep it running. I'll be quick." Already on the path. Over her shoulder. "What's dinner?"

"French fancy or farm less-fancy."

"French din-din, farm breakfast if we get out of bed."

"That's why they invented brunch."

Layla zoomed inside. Shift gears. Lynn checked back in with herself as she prepped her bag. Last looks: anything Kingston not Kingsbury. Nothing. Good.

Layla: you are good to go.

And go, go, go, they did. Off the 340, found their way into Virginia and onto the scenic Harpers Ferry Road. Down through Louden. Down through Mechanicsville. Off the main road into a rolling country of hidden farms. Hunt country. One of those. Stonehouse Inn and Farm—first class country luxury—all set and waiting for them.

Never asked for Elmin or Aydin and she pretended not to notice. The main manor—1834, 1930s rebuilt, 2004 full restoration/upgrade. Rooms, suites, pool, restaurants—screamed wedding; they took a golf cart to one of the four themed "cottages."

Brain hiccup. Just had to book the one looks like the dwarf twin of Silas's North Vista Outhouse. Coincidence. Don't flinch.

"And your rate for checking in forever?"

Inside. The amenities tour. Roman, perfect gentleman, tipped their "weekend butler" and the bellhop carrying their hardly-anythings, discreetly and well when he thought she wasn't looking.

Pop! the champagne. Pop the first question: "So, Roman, does this make us a couple?"

"Are you into the 'official' of it all?"

Right now, your security fucks are raping my home and my office.

A throaty giggle. "I haven't been on the market very long and my first foray I get this?"

Meaning 'you.'

Yep, there it is: a genuine blush. God, he's sweet. Ease him back.

"Soon as you count your Lotto numbers, you sign that winning ticket; make positive it's..."

Wait for it.

Roman. "Official. I like the sound of that." He snuggled up next to her on the sofa. Lynn rubbed her face against his black cashmere turtleneck over his chest, his heart, between the royal blue lapels of his blazer. A tender finger. He tilted her chin. They kissed. She shuddered. He pulled back.

"What's up? I see tears."

"Shut up and keep kissing Layla, you colossal idiot."

♔ ♔ ♔

AFTERNOON INTO the evening. Roman spent it trying to hide his constant phone checking. Either Layla would clear or not; since they'd gotten to a "country inn weekend" point, embassy security preliminaries on Layla Kingsbury must have come up shiny-happy-squeaky-clean.

He's asking himself what's the stall?

She sat in front of the mirror in her private bathroom. Forest green raw silk, boho cocktail dress. Zip.

What did they find about sweet, innocent, tennis-loving Layla?

Knee-high boots. Zip.

Looked harder because of the townhouse. Found Layla's secret.

Some baubles. Some Bombay Sapphire for her bangle. A healthy shot from the short bottle before back-in-bag and some toothpaste.

Always give hunting dogs a scent to go after; send 'em barking up the wrong tree.

Tight suede jacket. Zip.

Make it an advantage.

She heard him, hushed, answer the phone. Heard the French patio door open. Heard it shut. Finished making up her face and making up Layla's mind.

Roman, there's something I need to tell you...

"I Googled Baku. Interesting city where you're from. Modern and ancient, all mixed together. And your beach resorts. Wow."

"Terrific place to grow up. You know, today is, at home, a holiday."

"What? You have a version of Thanksgiving?"

He grinned. "Well, yes, we are thankful, but no, it's called our National Revival Day. From 1988. Commemorates when protests broke out against the Soviet Union. It took three years, but we gained our independence in 1991."

"And you haven't looked back."

"You'd think. From where I sit—in my job—I see close ties between Azerbaijan and Russia. Still."

The server brought his Bulleit rocks. Her Sapphire martini. Roman swizzled the ice. He watched his ice twirl until it stopped. "It's a sad day for me, too."

"Why?"

Lifted his face. Met her eyes. "I lost my dad that same day. Accidentally killed in the riot."

"That's sad. I'm sorry. I lost my dad a few years back, but it was—" spread hands— "his time. Heart problems for years. Working at the post office did it, my mom always said." Sipped. "Was he political? Like you?"

"Not at all. Just wrong place, wrong time. It's strange, though, I'm here, I have my job, because of what happened to him. The family, his brothers—Aydin's dad and the others—elevated him to a kind of hero status." He drank. Considered the liquor again.

There it is: the "daddy" of it all. Father, hero, stranger: abandonment. Give it a nudge, Layla.

"He's proud of you—" cheek-turned-modesty— "looking down at who you've become. I bet. But you know that."

"My mother, she did everything for me and my three sisters. We didn't have it easy, but that story carried me and my job, that's my job, but—" a blast of teeth and warmth, face and eyes—"here I am with you."

She gave him back warmth for warmth. Lifted her glass. He touched it with his. "Roman, there's something I gotta tell you. I doubt it will be—hope it won't be—a big deal with you. And I can hear myself being weird about it already." Stuff with her hands.

Flighty.

Stuff with her hair.

Now a sexy flip.

"Shit: I'll say it. I'm divorced. Okay?"

Roman laughed. "So?"

That's relief. Now you're waiting for what you heard...

"He's an asshole. Wherever he is. He wasn't gentle. We'll leave that there."

Touch your cheek. Teeth on your bottom lip. His people have read the divorce by now.

"He had good lawyers. He is a talented lawyer. He got my inheritance. And he took our townhouse—threw me the fuck out—and then, for spite, he abandoned it. Leaves it empty. Like three years now."

Look at the relief.

"Did you do something? Make him go at you so hard?"

"Yeah. Caught him with a bimbo slut."

"Where is he now?"

Lynn downed her martini. Roman lifted a finger to the server. Signaled another round.

"Like I said. Don't know. Don't care. But I have a secret, and you can't tell."

"You have my word."

Here's the Layla Kingsbury they called and told you about.

"So, I always did our taxes, right? Every year, I'd cheat a little—yeah, 'bad girl'; it's easy—and I'd sock away a healthy chunk of cash-business cash. I was saving for—like an idiot—our dream house. Somewhere on a beach with a button for everything. Did this all ten years of our marriage. And a little here and there from our savings when I could. He didn't know to come after it and it'll never put me in a beach mansion, especially after that car Aydin put me into, but I won't ever have to depend on anyone ever again."

His eyes sparkled. "My mom would love you."

Doris. Fire. Diaries and Russian secrets.

"Layla, your eyes are doing that again."

"The better to see you with, my dear."

He placed a large hand over hers. Lynn added Layla's other hand to the bunch. "That promotion I was going for? I got it."

"That's great!"

"Shh-wait. We host a celebration at the embassy that combines Revival Day and, since this is America, Thanksgiving. On Thanksgiving. You're not a secret. I want you to come with me. I want to show you off. I'm feeling kind of lucky with you. I think we got a thing."

"I think we do."

"But this is the 'thing' thing. I'm in a security position. I do secret stuff. It's—don't worry about it—but I must ask you to do something."

Lustful eyes. "I pretty much say 'yes,' every time."

"Layla, this is serious. I need you to take a polygraph. It's so you can come inside the embassy; it's so I can keep seeing you."

"A what's that? Is that a lie detector test?"

Earnest eyes backing the smallest of nods.

"Hell, yeah. I just told you my biggest secret. Easy. But I have to ask, how fancy is Thanksgiving at an embassy? Is it like the movies?"

Roman lunged across the table. Held her face between his hands, pulling her up from her seat, all his pent worry flooding from him as passion in his lips.

Surprised guests at other tables, thinking they'd just become engaged, or maybe the gal's pregnant, or who knows, but it's gotta be something, put their hands together. Applauded. Everyone likes a happy ending. Lynn staggered. Face flushed. For real. A mischievous grin, she pinched the corners of her hem, took a theatrical bow.

2.

MICHAEL KINGSTON WORE HIS own tuxedo—person-ally/professionally—about the same number of times as it rains each year in the Algerian desert. The last thing a clandestine operator posting overseas thinks about is packing a tux. Maybe other services do it differently, but there are not a lot of bowtie parties, casinos, operas in the world of recruiting/running agents for the CIA. Bow ties and cummerbunds draw unwanted attention. The tuxedo Michael owned was a rental has-been he wore to a New York wedding. Some friend of Gwen's. The late fees—"I don't know—maybe I left it at the hotel!" "Here it is. Scrunched in the bottom of this suitcase—with everything else you didn't unpack"—made a buy-out the prudent way to go and, after some time and some moths, Paige repurposed it into her storage bin dress-up chest; wore it once to school to play Didi in an English class scene from *Waiting For Godot*.

This suit was not that suit. This suit was a single button, black vicuna, silk shawl collar, Kiton. Dior—"at least the collar's normal"—shirt, a belt with an ingot for a buckle, cufflinks and studs like a handful of—

"Soft-carat gold with traces of...nickel." Didn't quite sound like Roger Moore when spoken in Russian.

"Is that supposed to mean something to me?" Dr. Kiselyov asked.

"I only need one." Michael's Christopher Lee fared no better.

"How the hell'd she get the fit so perfect?"

"The two of you have been watching each other like a pair of cats. Go. You're embarrassing my apartment." The Russian doctor held up the ever-ready Aeroflot ticket. "You got straight to the airport after the party and, looking like that, you'll get champagne and caviar the entire way home."

Michael pinched his warty pumpkin cheek. "I'll see you after the ball."

"Don't let her Chechen show you the view from the roof!"

♛ ♛ ♛

THE VIEW FROM LULU's penthouse balcony, off her sunken (in opulence and overflowing) living room, was to die for. Her Chechen led Michael to her. She stood on a glass platform twenty-five stories above Presnensky on the Third Ring Road.

"Enjoy it while it lasts."

"The view?"

Lulu nodded without looking at him. "That construction? With all the work lights?"

"All twisted."

"Yes. Evolution Tower. It will look like a strand of DNA when it's completed. My view of the river will be gone."

She turned and leaned the small of her back against the chrome rail atop her glass balcony wall. Faced him. She wore a Cristallini evening dress of purest white that enhanced the living brilliance, shining with the inward light from her pale complexion. Mermaid cut, as Michael was learning she favored, with hand-sewn Italian applications—shoulder, neckline, chest and sides—embroidered to resemble pine boughs, infused with Swarovski crystals. Her cape sleeves, elbow-cut, fell gracefully along the length of the dress. They billowed in the cold November night wind. Except for the champagne flute she kept and the one she placed in Michael's hand, they were alone.

"I'm early?"

"No."

"You said dinner 'party.'"

"Don't underestimate the two of us."

Michael raised his glass. Lulu matched the gesture. "I hope you let the caterer know."

That impertinent smile as she looked away. Looked at the night. Looked at the far edge of the black dome of night. He muttered, "You look beautiful." And she said, "I'm not allowed to do much with my time that's useful. Cooking is one thing I do that is. Or can be if you have someone to entertain."

He stepped beside her. Their shoulders brushed. He pulled away before she could.

"While I was waiting, I was thinking. We've possibly had an equal number of thoughts, you and I, in our lifetime. You a few days older, a few more, and I was thinking, at the beginning, same doctor, same hospital, same nurses, I'm sure—our first thoughts, except for our mother's touch, must match."

"Freakish."

He got a genuine laugh out of her. She wet her lips with champagne. "Do you miss your daughters?"

"Of course I miss them."

"Why don't you go home to them?"

She sure knows how to ruin a moment.

"What you're doing doesn't matter to them. You matter to them."

"It might matter to the world."

"It doesn't. Has it ever? Your work—saved the world?"

"A couple times. Not the entire world, but a great number of people. Brought justice for a great number lost. I did that."

"Are you very brave?"

Michael stared at her. Wondered why he wasn't angry, being taunted.

She means it. Really wants to know.

What do I know?

"In any situation I may have come out of looking brave, I never thought about it. Maybe it's those moments of selfishness and cowardice, cruelty—I've been known to display, lots more than any heroism—but it's those moments where you just don't be that. Now you make me think about it. I've never been brave. Thanks a lot. Just drew a line at those other human qualities. Temptations. I don't know. What did you cook?"

She drank. She looked at his face. Her lips smiled against the rim of her glass. She didn't share why she smiled. Swallowed, and it was gone.

"My husband never drew that line. He wrote poetry—"

"Russians and their poetry."

"Young Russian men at universities have a sickness for that and young Russian woman are not their nurses but the disease. No, he never drew that line away from selfishness—and *all* poets are selfish—and me," she raised her arms at her tower penthouse, "I am the same. But cruel. Do you love your wife?"

"Want to go inside? Get out of this wind?"

"'Go inside,' 'Get out of the wind?' 'What's it you cooked?' Michael, are you a hungry little bird?"

"Honey, I'm starving. And 'no,' I don't love her, I didn't for years, and I lied to her about that and she lied to me and maybe that's why I don't want to face my girls. I showed them a real crappy example for the kind of man to marry. Now, can we eat something?"

What the fuck is wrong with you? Ten minutes here and you're flapping your mouth.

Lulu took his arm. Leaned into his shoulder. "Let me feed you. And don't be a coward. If it's awful, you'll tell me."

♛ ♛ ♛

SHE CALLED HER PENTHOUSE her *Ostrov Radosti*. Her Island of Joy. An open-floored, three-story living space constructed of glass and chrome, tubular steel and guy-wire fencing. Sterile and unapologetic, it found its beauty in the hard angles and gentle ellipses of its prisonlike skeleton. Prisonesque mood. Lulu animated the skeleton with a design palette Michael remarked was nothing so much as "living inside a cappuccino as it's being made." Tones and textures of the darkest almost-black beans, the glossy brown of hot poured espresso, the beige of cooling coffee mixed with cream. The delightful part of cappuccino, the white of the foam and this, with her genetic condition, was Ludmila Sidorova. They dined at a serious black table; a black chrome pedestal base that held the center length of a single walnut tree, massive and more than one hundred years old when killed and set into a rectangle of sharp-edged black resin.

Surrounded by twelve chairs, uncomfortable in appearance but congenial swoop backed, and time passed gently in them. Lulu insisted Michael take the head of the table while she scooted as close to his chair as the corner allowed.

He had never experienced a personally prepared meal as delicious and satisfying and invigorating as this one presented him by Lulu (served by her silent Chechen), nor would he ever remember any of the vast and invisible epicurean complications she described while they dined. Nothing that came from her kitchen in small course after course appeared any more marvelous than any gourmet meal eaten, seen, read about in his lifetime; there were no new or unusual tastes. No potion or drug or fantastical secret ingredient. But with each morsel that he consumed, a sense of calm marvelousness grew inside him and connected him to his companion. The final plate vanished; Michael realized this meal was unique. A singular lifetime experience.

If the meal had perhaps been less appealing, Michael would have left the conversation.

"I must apologize. I asked you about your wife. Your children. I don't know you. You don't know me. This was rude. My unintentional nature—to be direct—to speak my mind/heart as they open to immediate thought and feeling. Have you arrived yet?"

"I'm sorry. Arrived? Where?"

"To the year where feelings don't feel inside, like they did when we were young. To capture them, or, better, to keep them captured, I need to say them aloud. Make them hard, like they once were. Vigorous and godlike. Instead of soft and lazy like they prefer to be now."

Paige. The old tux. St. Pancras Hall auditorium.

"Habit is a great deadener."

"That's what you think."

"I think nothing about feelings. Zip."

"Except lust. You still feel that?"

"Are you coming on to me?"

"Not kinetically."

Forthright. Inscrutable. Unpredictable.

Lulu.

She told him of her husband. Of Maxim Sidorov, her poet-lover, pre-law Kutafin Moscow State Law University classmate. They married. Too young, too on-fire. "Too happy and hopeful for our own good. I graduated to a childless campus apartment; Maxim conquered the law."

She poured herself wine. Reached to pour him, he waved her off. She poured through his fingers. "Drink it," she said, then recited. "There are three epochs to reminiscences/And the first is like a day gone by... In a deaf suburb there's a solitary house./Where the winters are cold and the summers hot/Where letters, like old flames, smolder/And portraits change in the stealth of night."

Michael braced as if from a blow.

Foxtail Farm? Doris? How could this be possible?

Candlelight flickered upon her rouged cheeks. She appeared unreal. The firelight untrue. If she noticed his reaction, it only relaxed her more deeply.

"To clarify, Maxim did not write those lines. His poetry was roses, hearts, and flowers—sometimes a cloud shaped like a cupid, sometimes shaped like a 'bouncing ball' which seemed ripe with meaning when I was nineteen."

"Did you write that?"

Ask!

"Did Kolya Yurenev?"

She drank, languid and amused. "Uncle Kolya is many things; all of them *not* poetic. Anna Akhmatova in 1945. After surviving the siege of Leningrad. To me, she is our most important modern poet, but I am wandering. Poetry has nothing to do with my story."

She explained to Michael that neither she nor Maxim was involved by/involved themselves in her father or Kolya Yurenev's KGB/FSB/Kalaydoskop business. But an uncanny prescience on Maxim's part—read "Kolya"—a series of investments into worthless wild lands, turned out to be rich in manganese. Soon, Maxim was rubbing elbows with the oligarchs. One, if not the youngest, to emerge in the 1990s.

"Wealth and the power of wealth. Greed and the gaudiness of grand excess." She flung her arms wide, high priestess of a splendid, empty temple.

Hands supple. Fingers drooping. Undulating. Leaves at the ends of lissome birch boughs in slow, soft, summer breeze.

"The gossip papers crowned me Princess Lulu, and Maxim flew high until Maxim flew off a discotheque rooftop. The mines are gone. The wealth, too—except what it takes to keep Maxim's widow inside the shell of the lifestyle we once enjoyed together. Now, when I am noticed in society, the columnists and celebrity news commentators call me simply 'Lulu' because everyone fears to put 'Prisoner' before my name."

"Who's holding you in your golden cage?"

"Maxim knew nothing about mining. Manganese. The rise of Putin's oligarchs was a threat to my father and Uncle Kolya."

"Kalaydoskop."

"It is called. They used Maxim to spy on the oligarchs. This was the time of the Nord Stream pipeline. They were desperate to control it. Kalaydoskop desperate to see them not. Maxim made a wretched spy. I hope you are much better."

"I won't betray my country."

"You tell Kolya that. He'll tell you, Silas Kingston is a great hero; were he known, beloved by our great motherland. It is all relative, I think. Putin looks at it that way. Uncle Kolya made him see energy is a stronger force than military might. The oligarchs see that money for the sake of money is stronger than both. Putin bets both sides—"

"Kalaydoskop and the oligarchs."

"—yes. Winner takes all. Like they took Maxim and Alina."

"Who's Alina?"

Lulu tilted back her head and laughed once. "Did you think I remained childless? Albinism is not linked to sterility."

Shit. I know the path she's leading me. Shit.

"I never thought—I never meant to imply anything like—"

"*Mikhail Nikolaevich*, I'm only teasing you. I'm trying not to tell you. You've eaten a plum, I imagine?"

"I'm not following you."

"Of course you are; you know exactly what I just asked you and you had an answer immediately as I spoke the words."

"You were telling me about your daughter."

"It's the sweetest fruit. To me. But it is impossible to eat one without scraping your teeth on the stone. Unless you wait until it's perfectly ripe. Too soft to sell in a store. It has to have dropped from the tree. Then you pick it up—" Michael mesmerized to her acting it out— "and you suck the pit out first, spit it, then the fruit, which only remains falling through your fingers, because it was half-rotten to begin with; sticky pulp you shove into your mouth where it dissolves, lost of everything that gave it shape and beauty.

"I had a daughter. Maxim and I. She would be fourteen now. Alina. The one no one will speak of. I let myself overripen in this life. I fell from the tree and warmed in my sweet rot. Alina's life was sucked from me. Spit from life. The same night my husband was murdered. They excluded me solely because of Kolya Yurenev. Your father. I am a prisoner. I am untouchable. The victim of an unspeakable crime. I continue to die from the loss of them both every day."

Michael took the wine bottle. Poured for both of them. "I won't kill anyone for you."

"Please. I have my own assassin. Tomorrow, return to the Victor Vasnetsov House. Study the paintings. Find which holds my heart and we shall make our trade. It is very simple."

Before Michael could answer, Lulu left the table. Around a corner, then she appeared on the floating stairway. Ascended planks of suspended natural cut sandalwood. Michael watched her disappear into a glass-walled master suite, his vision of her obscured by height.

The Chechen met Michael at the door. He held a pebbled black leather duffel. "All your things from Dr. Kiselyov." He held it out until Michael, bemused, took it. He continued. "Other hand."

Michael held it out. The Chechen dropped his black gold wedding band onto Michael's open palm.

"I'll show you to your rooms."

Michael looked at the front door. Looked at the vicious old bear. Nodded he proceed. "Did the doctor say anything?"

"Said you were underfoot. Like a dog."

"He said that before. Not very nice."

The man showed Michael his room. Gestured he enter. "A dog is faithful. Devoted to pleasing and will fight to the death to protect those they love. They choose love through kindness and faith. Keep that in mind while you stay with her."

When he lay on the bed, Michael smiled to himself, humor pushing away his total bewilderment.

Most poetic threat against my life I've ever heard.

He put his ring on the bedside table. He shut the light.

Sunday, November Eighteenth

1.

AFTER ONE IN THE morning. Melody awakened to a groan. Hal returned home. Returned to their bed. Undressed. His side. On the edge, staring at his hands. Her hand on his back.

"You okay?"

"I didn't mean to wake you."

"I didn't hear you come in. What's wrong with your hands?"

"These hands. Messed them up a little."

"How long they let you out for?"

"I deploy on this thing tomorrow evening."

"I'm glad they gave you one night." Melody switched on her light. "Let me see your paws."

Hal displayed his hands. Front. Back. Individual fingers. Had some stitches, base of his left thumb. A burn—second degree, mostly healed, goopy with silver sulfadiazine—back of his right. Bunch of cuts on his fingers. Bunch more minor burns.

"What kind of training they have you doing? French fries?"

A chuckle. "I can't tell you, but I've shredded a shit-ton of nitrile gloves getting the hang of what no one's supposed to know." Another grunt. "It's the throbbing that's impossible. I can't get where one hand or the other isn't touching something."

She pressed the side of her face between his shoulder blades. "They let you take something?"

"Ibuprofen. I told 'em I didn't need the other."

Melody folded back her covers. Feet on the floor. "I got the other. Hold on."

Returned with the Vicodin. Water. Pill popped. Eyes met. Memories/moment/future: all there; direct current. Simultaneous, "Hi."/"Yeah, hi, you."

And then Melody knelt on the floor. Right up to him, hands to knees to open legs. Gave it a try. Hal held his breath. Looked at her; looked away; didn't know where to look; didn't want to fail. Not again. Tried to think/help. Tried not-to-think, if that'd help. A bunch of *God, please*, inside his head. And it happened.

And he felt stupid because he felt his eyes burn and a lump in his throat.

And then instinct, history, first-time-every-time, full current: AC and DC. Total confidence. "Come up here, baby. I got this."

Hands hurt like hell. Might as well been afire. Couldn't care less. Hal lifted the love of his life/grand total magnitude of his life onto him. His lap. She smiled in his face. Right up in his eyes. Teeth clicked before lips cushioned before tongues spoke warm wordless language. Curls off Melody's forehead tickled his nose, as he adjusted and she looked down and moved her hand. Made things right. Perfect smooth—that Melody smile: brighter than the lamplight, and she lowered all the way, pressed, ground herself onto him-into-her. "I missed you, my man. God." She stretched her back and let him do his part. "Yeah-hi-*you.*"

***

WHEN THE TWINS GOT UP, bounced from their room, Melody ducked from her bedroom. Found Charlotte and asked if she would take care of their cereal. Instructed: no TV, put them in their jackets and kick them outside to play until she and Hal came down. Charlotte blushed. Thought she knew what had already happened three times was yet to come. The boys glowed at word their daddy was home; Charlotte enlisted Leigh, and—

"Did Paige come home last night?"

"*They* are still asleep." Charlotte.

"She doesn't like it when we come to the door." Leigh.

Hal was fast asleep. Melody squared up. Centered herself. Pulled a chair, like Silas had with her, up beside Hal and waited for him, listening to the children's stampede galumphing down the stairs.

Leigh: Good morning, Grandma. Three-two—

It echoed back, "Morning, Gramma Doris!"

Leigh's high pitch did the trick. Hal's eyes opened.

"Wow. That thing knocked me out."

"Which."

"Exactly. Was that the boys, too?"

"Went down with the girls."

A moment like a glimpse before going over a cliff. Wish it was bottomless. Go on forever. But that bottom is there, and it's far and the impact will devastate. Her sigh was like the wind coming up from the gorge. "Hal, I know you're shipping out, but this week—"

"I know. I'm missing Thanksgiving, I'm..." His words slowed. "Sorry about that. This one's open-ended. Too." Zero energy by the time he finished. Everyone's got an "over the edge" face. He'd seen hers before, but not like this. Pretended a driveway crack, a pothole, not the "you don't climb out of this one" face she affected. At least her faced was warning him. "Why are you scaring me?"

"Because I'm scared."

"But *not* about me."

"No. You know that. I gotta leave town, too." Went fast. "I'm flying to Alabama. My dad's being let out of prison."

His words came in a rush. All you can get in as you plummet into the Grand Canyon of blindside-surprise/disbelief/denial. "You're what? Prison? What are you talking about? Your father's in Arkansas. Isn't he? You have no relationship with him since—*you* said—you were eighteen and left home." Breathe.

Let him go, let him go; let him get it all out.

Logic/conclusions/terminal acceptance. "You've been in contact with him? Prison? Alabama? Melody! How long's this going on? *What's* going on? Who the hell is this guy? Why's he in prison? You only said he was a—a *shit* father. A bastard. You hate him. Why would you have to go? What the fuck?! You've been lying to me?!"

"Not telling is not lying. But yes. Maybe it is. And I have. That way."

"Jesus!" He lurched from bed. Went halfway to the bathroom. Over her shoulder, watched him stop. Turn. Grabbed the back of her chair. Just watched. Head tilted up, back over her shoulder. Old terror flooded.

Mama glows joy.
Grips her chairback.
"It's a statewide chain. Dresses to start, but some blouses, the slacks. That's my name—Roberta—and our shared name, Kelso—"
Her head snaps profile under his hand. Mama pretends it isn't happening. "I'll hire seamstresses—"
I see a hundred tiny dots of blood.
"We'll get a bigger place—"
His reach incredibly long.
Melody fought for peace. Hal threw himself off her chair. Two steps stomped to their bed. Threw himself hard, sitting. "Lying is fucking lying. I don't know you right now." Voice cracks. "You know how much that hurts?"

Melody nodded.

"Don't agree with me!"

"He was a criminal. And a drunk. And he drank worse stuff that made him crazier and crazier—"

"Your mom. She still in the picture, too?!"

Mama hanging onto her chairback. Pink drool-string hanging from her lips. She looks down. Eyes wide. I see the whites.

"You can stop drinking your poison—you call it that—and be creative, and paint—"

Mama's hand. Fingers crooked. Tips caress his cheek.

"And you can spread your legs for more strangers the minute I'm gone?"

"Boone Kelso, you know that isn't true."

Bone snapping. Mama howling.

Tremors coursed. Melody summoned them to shake her head. "I told you. He abused her. She died in a fire. I left him as soon as I *was* eighteen. He *was* in Arkansas. But he was a criminal. I told you—"

"You *never* told me that!"

"Not that! That I was from Arkansas. When we met. He was arrested for crimes he committed in Alabama."

He read the avoidance on his wife's face. "Your mother, Melody."

She shook her head. Vehement. Forceful. Pleading eyes.

"You're lying about that, too. You are. I can see you are."

Because she never cried, the tears running from her eyes, rolling down Melody's cheeks, focused her mind. Warm-wet-cooling. Absorbing in her cheeks. Her tears put the brakes on the crash of uncontrolled emotion. Arrested jumbled thoughts so she could select one. The most honest thing she could say. "Even with you. My love. My heart. I can't share that."

Impossible for him to guess/imagine anything close to the circumstances of Melody's reality, her intimate and exact involvement, Hal knew, as intimately as he knew his wife; he knew, because it was part of who he was, and the ultimate endgame he played to in everything he did; "that," as she expressed it, bore a definition written on his soul. Kill/killing/killed. The difference between loving/committed/devoted life partners and soulmates is that the deepest corners and canyons of two souls find perfect symmetry when they meet as mirrors.

He didn't wipe her tears. He didn't hold her. "I don't know what to do with this."

Melody didn't bother to wipe her tears either. Finished, the last of them cooled on her cheeks and felt, to the oblique surprise the morning had brought her to and the way she viewed it, inspiriting.

Out of the chair and back. Her phone. An Arkansas number. Texts starting with—

"Coming soon, child. 4u & 4 them. Better have found it."

A dozen more below.

Melody watched Hal's expression change. He stared at her as he would a stranger. "He wants to hurt me, Hal. Hurt all of us. Papa most of all."

Hal's eyes widened, whitened, rolled; in a dog, they're called "whale eye." Stress. Threat perception. "How would he know where we are?"

Melody reached for him. Not his wounded hand. Put her fingers on his thick forearm. He looked at her dark and slender hand. Her ring. Laid his other hand over it. "How does he know?"

"His name is Boone Kelso."

"Do I know that name?"

"B-o-o-n-e. Before he lost his mind, or let the evil always there take over, he was, for a sad, short time, famous. He painted portraits."

"Mom's painting. Does Dad know?"

Melody didn't smile, but a tiny pursing of her lips became the first speck of blue winking between the storm clouds that crowded and threatened their entire horizon—Melody raised her eyebrow.

Hal said, "Stupid question. Has he said anything?"

"In his way. He said this would be our most brutal winter. That you and I would see his lambs safe through the storm."

"Clear as mud. As usual. I wish you wouldn't go."

"Me too. But I'm going."

"I feel terrible about leaving."

"Hal: go. You always come back."

Which was the precise moment their twins' voices flew to their windows like the scream of startled birds scattering in flight.

2.

*N*EVER AGAIN WOULD S*ILAS* *Kingston allow a dog inside the gates of Foxtail Farm...*

The Claypoole Hound of St. Mary's County (and Hollywood, though not the St. Mary's Hollywood, but the one on the opposite coast), was a dog breed unrecognized by the American Kennel Club. In the woods where it still thrived (due to the irascible Claypoole descendants' defiance of longstanding, unenforced, forgotten/ignored ordnance and their unconditional love for the family's Frankensteinian creature), and along roadsides where it would sometime still appear, it was puzzlingly recognizable as something that wasn't something else. Antique accidental mismanagement and a more contemporary *noblesse oblige* to its propagation that, with hurled bottles and some remember hearing it was hurled lead, defied legal/ordered eradication made for the animal that, promised on Independence Day, Silas delivered to his twin grandsons the Sunday morning of the week of Thanksgiving.

From a distance, with one eye closed, a squint of the other, one could say, it was not the golden retriever or Labrador pups, the charcoal black French bulldog, or one of the four, snowbally Samoyed doglets Melody, several times, had taken the twins to acquaint them-selves/roll-around with at the *Meet, Play, Love* puppy store opened last year in the Wildewoode Shopping Mall, St. Mary's County, City of California, a weekend resort town of almost eleven thousand (if you choose to count the young folk who grow up and move away, and top that off with the workers who commute in for tech/defense work at the Patuxent River Naval Air Station), a place you could miss if driving fast between Hollywood and Lexington Park.

One closed eye. Other, squinted. At about thirty yards... Silas emerged from the overgrown fields, a dog dancing on a brand-new leash, Silas not minding at all. Yes, a person knowledgeable of dog breeds might say his frolicsome companion was an American foxhound puppy, about a year in age. With one eye closed, the other squinted, at a distance of thirty yards, it appeared sleek and rangy as the first pack of hounds introduced to Maryland by Governor Robert Brooke almost fifty years before the rise of Foxtail Farm.

Twenty yards from the porch steps—where Melody nursed her guilt and restrained Little Silas and Jack who, since they couldn't break free, lifted their faces to the cold November air and bayed—at this distance, it be-came noticeable this American foxhound had picked up, somewhere along its bloodline, some terrier in a mantle of curls bristling its neck and front shoulders; this dis-tance, its skull bore less a slope than any modern breed of dog. Its oscillating, drool-tossing head harkened back to the domesticated wolves of the original Piscataway, Governor Brooke experimented with to failure three hundred and sixty years prior.

Ten yards to go. Silas released the leash. The bounding boundless fren-ergy cartoon-skidding just-up-to, but not-crashing-into-the-boys animal allowed Melody an understanding that this dog was not a puppy; she knew in her heart, as the dog lapped at her twins' faces and in the grins of the circling girls (who'd come yelling from television inside), that this earnest creature had been making its way to their family for three or four years since weening from its mother's teat.

It eased, softened, the unwanted hardening of her heart to her foul predicament, and Melody smiled at Silas. "I sure hope the puppy mill gives back my deposit."

"Dear angel, have you ever known me not to keep my word?"

Hal had been watching through the porch shutters—keeping distance, keeping his counsel, keeping his kit at the ready waiting for his car—came outside.

He dropped a wounded hand to Melody's shoulder. Silas knew at an instant she had allowed her secret a sparkle of the light of truth, so often absent in his family home. No one noticed him clench his fist three times at his side.

Hal jerked his chin at his father. "A Claypoole, huh?"

"That's right, son." Silas. Level eyes/smile paused. "You have a problem with that?"

"I always wanted one."

"You weren't ready." Silas shifted his glance between his son and Melody. "Neither his brother nor the gir—"

"Don't dare say it."

"Lynn. These lambs are."

Hal blew out his cheeks—*pffhhp'd*—joined the children, getting in the scrum with the dog.

"I've never heard of a Claypoole."

Hal reached in. Removed the leash. Twins, girls, Hal, dog tumbled into the old tournament field yard.

"Like the old family up the way?"

Silas looped the leash. Watched his bloodline, the only thing real that he cared about, at play. Melody saw the goodness he felt and tried to stay positive with her feelings, press back her fear about leaving that night. "Silas, don't keep me in suspense."

"The original Claypoole farm was much larger than Foxtail Farm. They were here at least thirty years before any Kingstons, but—" he nodded at the space beside her; she patted it and he sat— "They backed the wrong horse in the Revolution. Fled to Canada. Left a son and his wife behind while they waited in New Brunswick. Let the British to make quick work of Washington and those rascally Declaration of Independence upstarts. That generation Claypoole would have lost it all were it not for our twins' grandfather Silas so many Roman numerals removed, who took title of all of his property and, bygones being bygones, leased it back when the Claypoole brood returned—"

"'Property.' Including their slaves?"

Silas's eyes gleamed, penetrating into hers for an instant. "It does. Yes. Not this story. But ask me one day about Cupid Williams if you want to curl your hair even tighter."

They pretended he wasn't baiting her.

"What I'm trying to say—and this gets back to the *dog*." His eyes penetrated again. "I'm trying to explain how we get from there to here. That." Pointed at the dog Charlotte already had chasing and returning a stick.

"Our Kingston ancestors cared for their land, but not so much for their kennels, which already carried crossbred Foxhounds from the original colony batch."

"Crossbred?"

"With Indian wolf-dogs."

"Wolfhounds."

"Nope. None of that Russian crap. Real half-wolf/half-dog beasts. The pack ran loose all over this peninsula, and there were actual wolves, still. And other furry bystanders; Kingstons kept Welsh terriers for generations, and the Claypooles got in with them, too. And, anyway, here's your slaves again, Claypooles backed Abe Lincoln a little earlier in the Civil War than others in these parts appreciated—a hundred years after the Scrapefoot Williams massacre, they'd gotten squared away on the morality of 'property'—and again, they lost everything except those few rundown acres they still have."

To make a soulmate, the inscribing of souls must go back like railroad tracks laid by both bloodlines for your trains to meet.

She said, "That old, falling-down house. Those come-and-go trailers—"

"No going. Those trailers come, and stay for years. Until they pull them apart for scrap or repurpose for animals." Silas shook his head. "They used to wear powdered wigs there and pinch snuff, and the men would paint their faces and paint little beauty marks right here." He tapped her cheek. Place where the owl scare had faded. "But the *one thing* they kept throughout, long as they could, were their original hounds. For a while, Claypoole hounds—the Historical Society has an entire book on them—were *the* hunting dog to lead your pack. But all those political troubles. The mixing in the forest." He laced his fingers and padded his palms together. "Those half-foxhound half-wolf dogs weren't half as good. As the Claypoole farm decreased in size, that pack a'dogs grew larger until about the time of the Depression. Finally, the state of Maryland came in. Was going to kill them all. And I'll tell you this and this means a lot about character.

"No Claypoole—no matter how inopportune they were politically, how tarnished their stanchion, their social reputation collapsed with their economic downfall, how their name became scorned as it is today—no Claypoole ever once harmed or let anyone harm their useless but ever-loved Claypoole hounds. Now I don't know how they came to it. Maybe they'd always known but didn't see the value in it until circumstances made it imperative, but this crazy dog they'd invented could train to do anything other than hunt."

"Like what?"

"Like tricks. They bought time with the county—Baltimore ordered them to euthanize the dogs—and crated some up. Took them to Hollywood. The faraway Hollywood. Sold them. The Silent Era is filled with Claypoole dogs. And that drew Ringling Brothers and Barnum and Bailey. Pulled in the regional circuses. But like Claypooles did with their farm, they kept selling what they had and didn't think about making a going concern of it so they went back down to just a few and the next generation, back in the sixties, cared even less and let the dogs run wild again in the woods and it's always been known—that's what Hal was talking about, the kids were dying, especially the boys, for a trick dog—that if you catch one, or you go knock on Claypoole's door or their trailer wherever they live now, who's ever still feeding them, that dog's yours."

"Did you knock on the door for this one?"

Silas laughed. "You know that's not me."

Melody grinned. "How long it take you to catch this one?"

He swelled a bit. Grinned back and this was the Silas she remembered long after he was gone. "I've been coaxing that dog to this leash since end of July. And look at that." He nodded to the grass.

Hal held his arms in a hoop. Presented to the dog. Wagged his head to his boys. "Get around, get around, get-around-an'-call-it!"

They scrambled. "What do we call it?"

"We'll figure it out later! Just clap. Motion with your hands. Watch this, girls." He clicked his tongue to keep the dog's attention. "It'll jump. I promise you."

Silas yelled: "Its name is Beaumont!"

"C'mon, Beaumont! Jump!"

The dog sprang with knowing delight; lips whiffling, brown ears flopping.

Silas didn't look at Melody when he said, "I'll watch the boys, but do you think it's your best move to confront him?"

Ice blood. Electric panic. Dead, immobilizing fear. Melody's mouth an "O."

"...Didn't mean to eavesdrop, but you leave the door open like I've told you not to at night; I was out of toast the other morning when you were on the phone."

"You know who he is?"

"Since the day you captured Hal's heart. How could I ever forget your ten-year-old face?"

"He swore you never saw us."

"You saw me. Didn't you think I looked back?"

"We were so frightened, Papa. That day. Of him. Here."

"Do you know what he's after?"

Silas pulled the leash in lengths and loops of leather between his fists. "In my line of work, I've dealt with some of the worst characters strutting across the world stage. We designate them evil. And many, many, many of them foster it. Breed it into their followers. Evil ideologies that forgive the unforgiveable. Boone Kelso isn't like that. If he were to kill, say, me. Or you. All of us, it wouldn't be from a corrupting ideology. From the power or the treasure or vengeance he deludes others—" Silas took her shoulders, pressed his forehead against hers—"*you* with. He doesn't care. Wrong word. He feels nothing about that. His evil is pure evil. The kind God banished to Earth. You know that. I think you've witnessed it more profoundly than I can explain it."

Melody pulled back. "I can't let him come here. Out of the blue."

"You can't go and kill him. You weren't thinking that when you booked your flight. So, there's only one other reason you'd go."

She nodded.

He knows. He's okay with it. Not afraid.

"Go inside. Right now. Go look at Doris, who'll help you, because regardless whatever else he did, and however he did it, your father captured a bit of both your souls in that canvas."

"What happened that day? When we came to deliver the portrait. The day I saw you."

"I told you. I saw you."

Silas released her.

Melody slipped inside as the boys and Hal cheered and Paige with Clive—the pair still thick with late night lack of sleep—passed her on the steps with muted greeting. And then Paige saw it. The kaleidoscope turned—

"We got a dog?! Holy shit!"

—and she was the kid that still grew inside her, and she rushed past Silas who growled, "Hey, watch that potty mouth," whose eyes traded sidelong glances with the British spy left beside him, and Beaumont the dog jumped through Hal's arms with Jack shouting: "He did it! Mom, did you see?! Mom? Where's mom? Ah, shoot! She missed it." And Silas said, "I didn't." He jogged to them from the porch. "Let's see what else you can get him to do." Lowered his voice to Hal. "Was it worth the wait?" Hal nodded and because he was the most innocent child Silas had, felt comfortable asking, "It's okay with Melody?" "It's O.K." Silas said, and Hal threw an arm around his father's shoulder and gave him a squeeze; Lynn—having cleared her tail on an SDR—roared through the gate in her new Mercedes to offer the girls rides and excuses herself from Thanksgiving and—like Hal had let Melody know before coming downstairs, while he showed her where his .38 snub nose lived, grab's-length from behind the pillows, from behind the mattress, from the fitting rigged on the headboard, how to load it, how to use it—maybe gone, up through Christmas. Silas looked to the moss-grown chapel where his wife lay buried below the stones they once wed upon and said in his heart both to Doris and to God, *Forgive us our sins as we forgive those who trespass against us*; he pictured Doris's face when, back from the Sylvanus Bench, he'd returned the original Beaumont to her arms. Tears in her eyes, she crushed the dog to her breast.

"There will never be another Beaumont."

"There never was." And he crushed himself to his terrible future.

The black iron carrion crow. Iron bone black in its beak. The weathervane swiveled without a breath of wind. Pointed to all that was unseen.

Monday, November Nineteenth

1.

MARSH, GERTZ, AND OSSANI. The A-bomb of Intelligence Community law firms; far as Gwen was concerned, she'd put them over target and all they'd dropped was a turd. Phone tag with the two junior partners she'd met. Brief discussions. Shallow interest. Real air of indifference. They'd called her in today. Smug, cheerful greetings—

As if any of us care.

Probably want me to write another check. For precisely nothing. Vampire bats. They want to ask for more cash, first thing I'm doing is getting my first ten grand retainer right back from them.

They put her alone inside a dim conference room. Left her alone with a bullshit, "We'll just get your files. Can we offer you a coffee? A soft drink?"

Make them work for it.

"Diet Dr. Pepper. The can's fine."

"I'm not sure we have that."

"Reeeeally." She rubber-banded that one. "Water. If not too inconvenient."

"Ice?" Ice. "Or bottled?"

"With. The recipe's not too difficult." Her chair had a great swivel, which she employed to face the windows. The rest of the world lay behind closed shades. She activated the hydraulic lever and sunk her chair to match her mood.

The door opened. She smelled Creed Aventus. Didn't turn at the scent. The First Lady's perfume, those who misted in the fragrance, wore it like an olfactory crown. "I'm seriously thinking I'd like the retainer I paid you returned."

"I'm seriously thinking that you, Mrs. Kingston, have not been honest with your team. For that—minus billed hours—I would be happy to return the balance."

Gwen recognized the voice. She'd watched YouTube senate hearings before choosing the firm. Her heart lifted. Her Cher-curls lifted—felt like it, anyway. She lifted, lifting the seat lever, turning, rising in her chair as she came back around and swelled her chest, in power red like a robin. Red breasts.

Senator Theresa Ossani was the cat who'd eaten more robins than anyone could count. Her sleek, blunt bob framed her heart-shaped face; her lips, Cupid's bow—if he fired a longbow—and her chosen words always flew from her lips with the kinetic energy of armor piercing arrows.

"Senator Ossani, I'm surprised to see you."

"But not surprised I've called you a liar."

Had Gwen been with Hal on Halloween night, she would have recognized the documents Senator Ossani placed on the broad table between them. Gwen did not recognize them; would have peed her pants had she been there. Put on her game face and responded. "I've not lied to anyone."

"Are you stupid, then? Or do you just not care to pay attention to the grave injustice you've been crying to your team about, that has nothing to do with your ex-husband being in anything remotely resembling a grave?"

"I see," said Gwen, because she couldn't think of anything meaningful. Or honest. Or dishonest.

I just want the money.

"These documents prove that Michael Kingston is alive and that your father-in-law, your brother-in-law and your sister-in-law—not Melody, but Lynn who works for Central Intelligence—have been working to defraud you and your daughters, and our government; you knew about it, have known all this time, and yet you keep crying—"

"I resent that. I don't cry. I'm not a child. All I want is—"

"As much money as my firm can get you. *This*, if you'd just be honest, will get you far more than measly back pay. Death benefit. Insurance pennies on the dollar. Is Michael Kingston alive and has your former family been covering this up? Yes, or no?"

"Excuse me." Gwen found a tissue in her purse. Dabbed her eyes. "Yes."

"That wasn't too hard, was it? Thank you."

The door opened. One of Gwen's "team." Carried both a glass of ice water and a can.

"Which would you prefer? Water or the Diet Dr. Pepper?"

"Oh. Water, please. I can't stand the sweet stuff. And yes-yes-yes, they're all in on it and it feels—you have no idea!—it feels like the weight of that Agency, my own government, is in a conspiracy on top of me."

The senator waited for Gwen's water to be served. Nodded the attorney from the room. Waited until the door closed behind him.

"Gwen, as a member of the Senate, I cannot work directly on your case. I can, however, help it if you trust me and share with me, in my official capacity, the privileged material of your case as I disassemble—and yes, he is running a vast conspiracy—Silas Kingston."

Glory hallelujah! I could kiss your lips and shove my tongue down your throat: I love you, bitch!

"If you think he deserves it, I could bring myself to cooperate. You have a pen? Wha'da I sign?"

"Tell me, Gwen, and then I'll need to step out and let you continue with your case attorneys—Tell me: have you heard about KALEIDOSCOPE?"

"The toy? One of the girls had one, I think."

"No. That would be too easy. Let's start paperwork, and I'll come back and swear you in as a witness to my committee—"

"How much money are we talking about?"

"Discovery in your lawsuit will provide me with the levers I need for my investigation. The lawsuit, Silas Kingston will try to settle; we will force him to a place he can't afford, at which point your digging will lead me to what I need. What that will expose will position you for suing the government. My firm will take that into eight or nine figures."

Gwen admired her. The look. The power. "Senator, may I ask, who does your hair?"

Senator Ossani rose from her chair. "This battle will see a hard fight. As soon as you can, you will move yourself and your three out of Foxtail Farm and prepare to live the rest of their lives apart from the Kingstons. Oh, and the droopy curls, the push-up bra: a perfect look for you. The girl from the wrong side of the bar who got an olive-sword in her eye."

2.

LYNN'S POLYGRAPH EXAMINER WAS an FBI early retiree. Wore a men's designer suit knock-off. The type bought three for two and two ties thrown in at one of those "Blow Out Sale!" locations that change their butcher paper "Everything Must Go!" signs more frequently than the contents/ownership of their stores that last on "clearance" for decades. Lynn knew the type: get the government training; the examiner prestidigitation; get some years of practical interrogation practice (the center-cut meat of their purview); save up for their own Truth Machine, then go private. With the notarized affidavit and the Society of Former Special Agents card the best of the hucksters pack, they can charge an extra per-hour bundle off that former three-letter cred, get paid every time they turn on their fanciest of fancies heart rate, blood pressure, respi-/perspiration machine for private and foreign suckers.

Silas maintained the polygraph machines, in and of themselves, were a hoax device. A fear factor crutch/distractor to amp up the effectiveness of subpar interrogators. One summer, back when Lynn and Michael were teens, Silas brought one home for kicks along with a mule-faced examiner. Meanest one Silas could find. Said it would be fun for them to play around with it.

Wasn't. It was frightening. Silas had the bastard browbeat the two of them two days a week for four weeks. It infuriated their mother, but Doris did nothing to stop it and, early on, Michael and Lynn agreed they wouldn't let their father or mule-face break them. But he always did.

"Thought you two—at least you, Michael—would've figured it out by now. The polygraph test is fake. Works on trickery and fear."

"But he's finding out our lies every time."

"Because, young man, you're throwing off deception indicators. You're making his job easy. Every time—"

Lynn got it: "Every time, we admit we lied. Or don't have an extra lie to escape the one we tripped on. I'm giving it away to him."

"That's right you are. Want to have him back a couple more times and kick his ass? Let me give you some tricks. Then I want to watch you whip this old mule."

That sounded fun. They agreed. He taught them all the physiological deceptive indicators, the way the body, eyes, and voice inflections are the real lie detectors. How they get you to volunteer information before the test; general questions you answer with general responses, make yourself like a sheep who believes that the lie detector is infallible at shearing you to the skin of the bare-naked truth. How to distinguish the control questions from the relevant and irrelevant questions; gum up the baseline by answering in a way that forces the examiner to modify that question. He/she modifies control questions enough, his baseline will never be accurate.

There were breathing tricks. There were tongue-biting and butt puckers. There were mental projections. "Prepared and practiced, vivid safe space or danger zone disconnected imaginings change heart-rate. Run mathematic tables." The idea wasn't to make a deception read as truth, it was to make your verifiable "true" answers as difficult to read as possible. This ruins the examiner's dominant position, forces him to begin straight interrogation, which causes aggression in the examiner and, "If you're capable of strong but controlled, as in 'placid' interrogation resistance, his machine reading will increase in inaccuracy. Just as you are being judged in your responses, the examiner is being judged for competency. You subliminally throw them off their game. They'll subconsciously work with you to get the exam back on track. Make the flutter box, flutter randomly until the examiner questions his own authority and capability. The other thing? At one point, the examiner will leave the room. Carry a marked-up section of your graph, like it's the holy grail, out of the room. Stay out. Sweat you. They'll come back and fail you. Always on your first go. They'll say, 'Think about what deceptive answers you gave today. Tomorrow you'll come back and be prepared to be truthful.'"

The mule-faced man came back to Foxtail Farm that summer three more times. Each of those times Lynn and Michael "beat" him. Years later, they realized that his pronouncement, and the confidence it gave them that polygraphs could be defeated using Kingston's methods, had forged their armor against future examinations.

Silas concluded their summer program/indoctrination with three silver bullet truths. Fact: the FBI discred-

ited the inventor of the "lie detector"; his real claim to fame, the only reason he's remembered, is that he created the comic book Wonder Woman. Fact: A man who believed plants could read thoughts instituted the CIA program. And ultimate fact: because polygraphs are not scientifically infallible, tests results are not admissible in court.

Whether entirely true, Michael and Lynn compared notes some years later and concluded that Silas had created in them a psychological resistance stronger than any examiner's tricks or traps. Not to mention skills. They admitted to each other that over the course of their professional careers they'd lied on their polys plenty. Enjoyed a laugh about that. When called up for their five-year "tune ups," while their colleagues were feeding and growing their pre-exam panic—freaking out if selected for random screening—Lynn and Michael waltzed in to play along.

"Funny," Michael once remarked. "They instituted the random screenings after Aldrich Ames's exposure as a Soviet spy, even though—since he always passed the screening—he's the reason they should eliminate it."

"I've been told we never had a single 9/11 suspect get deceptive readings. Why waterboarding became the main attraction."

"Sister, you are bad."

"Grade-A certified worst."

Lynn knocked on the door of the Downtown Washington Holiday Inn Express Roman had given her for her appointment. Three minutes late. On purpose.

The examiner in the three-for-two men's suit was a middle-aged woman—card carrying ex-FBI—who, legit or not, gave off an "I see right through girly-girls like you" butchy-butch vibe. She asked Lynn to take off her Burberry puffer. The examiner took the jacket into the adjoining room. Wasted five minutes, most certainly watching her on hidden camera. Back, she gave her spiel, asked the obligatory trap question— "Is there anything you'd like to get off your chest before we proceed?" And Lynn put up her first smoke screen— "Maybe. Do you have an example?"— got something inane back for her trouble, controlling the interaction outcome and breaking the efficacy of the dominance trap.

She wired Lynn up. "My name is Susie."

"Pleased to meet you, Susie. I'm Layla."

Susie announced they would begin with a calibration test. A blank sheet of printer paper. Susie wrote the numerals one through five in a column. Asked Lynn to choose one of them. This would be Layla's true number.

Lynn told her. "Four."

It's really two. And five.

Susie circled the two. Susie taped the paper to the wall behind her shoulder where Lynn couldn't help but always see it—

The circled 'four' of truth!

(Lie. Two and five are true.)

Mitigated.

Asked for Layla to lie to her about the number she chose. Read them one by one, questioned each number's "veracity" as it applied in relation to True-Four. Lynn lied about all of them.

So much for your calibration.

"Excellent responses."

Two hours into the interrogation, Susie abruptly left with a section of Lynn's read out. Shut the adjoining door harder than before. Audible. Almost a slam. Ten minutes later, Susie returned.

"I'm sorry, Ms. Kingsbury. But your answers indicate a high level of deceit. I explained that a civilian unused to this level of security and the serious nature of the polygraph, can mistakenly think they can be—" a keen, piercing eye— "dishonest in some of their responses. They have allowed for a second test. Can you be here promptly tomorrow morning at seven?"

Layla shuddered with worry while to herself, Lynn couldn't help but remember from her mother's most despised movie—

Who wouldst cross the Bridge of Death must answer me these questions three.

"I'm so sorry. I'm embarrassed. I swear I thought I answered everything honestly."

"This isn't about feelings, Ms. Kingsbury. This is about your dishonesty. Think hard tonight. It *will* come to you. We'll start there."

OF ALL THE WAYS to beat the polygraph, the best way of all is to plant, pre-exam, a rabbit garden. That's the little plot of delicious carrots and cabbages and turnips that have loose wires in their fence, little dug-out wriggle-in holes in the soft earth around. It goes right beside the real vegetable garden. The one that's ironclad/air-tight secure, four sides, top, and bottom. Layla's rabbit garden was the ex-husband, was his bimbo, was the empty townhouse, was the money squirrelled away and unreported in the divorce.

"Roman, she asked me all about that. All of it. Every which way."

"There must be something in your story you haven't been truthful about."

Lynn let the air go dead between their cell towers. "There might be something I left out. But it's not important, and I wasn't dishonest."

"It is important. What?"

Hello, darkness my old friend—a little more of the sound of silence, get his worst fears plop-plop follow the bouncing tennis ball, plop...

"Okay. But it meant nothing. And it was only one time."

"Layla: what?"

"After I caught him with his girlfriend, I went out and picked up a guy. Like a college kid. I had a one-night stand. I'm totally ashamed of myself..."

His laughter was genuine. Relieved. "I can just picture it. Poor guy."

"Poor guy? I rocked his world!"

"Do us a favor and tell them tomorrow. Then you can rock my world any time you want."

And she did.

The aggregate one hour they'd spent over both days on whether Layla Kingston worked for, contracted/associated with, had any interaction, took any money, volunteered with law enforcement/US or—and there was an extensive list—any other nation or private intelligence agency/company/program or its affiliates: never once put even the smallest kink in that bullish wonder woman Susie's magic Lasso of Truth.

Tuesday, November Twentieth

1.

Although the village idiot isn't depicted in any of Vasnetsov's four fairy tale paintings, by Michael's third visit to the Victor Vasnetsov Museum, the psychologically embattled, professionally embittered, metaphysically befuddled spy embraced his kinship with the hapless fool. The nutcracker security guard and the grandmotherly docent, who, as it turned out, was his wife, made fun of Michael for this—in Russian behind his back—although, since all three were aware he spoke and read the language, it was, as such, blatant laughter in his face. Still, when alone with the old woman, up in the artist's turret studio, her knowledge of and her love for Vasnetsov's once-secret works poured from her like honey and cream. With the occasional chestnut, profound with a certain and perpetual truth.

"Four paintings. Four princesses. My heart beats, imprisoned in one. When you tell me which, we will make our trade."

No wonder they jeer. I'm collecting intelligence from fairy tales.

Lulu-freakin'-Lulu.

It went without saying; Lulu envisioned herself as each one of them. On Monday, he'd dispensed with the main piece. *The Sleeping Tsarevna*. Banished princess, seven giants (instead of dwarves—how original), friendly woodland creatures, the promise of a prince (in the Russian version, a village idiot, though smarter than all the Prince Charmings combined). No huntsman, no heart. He did enjoy the lesson on anti-communist symbolism hidden in the painting, but having watched the DVD too many times with his daughters, knowing Lulu would consider his familiarity would incline him to choose it, he pushed "Snow White" aside in his imagination and had his little Baba Yaga friend—

Who knew? Doris's favorite evil witch, though a big-time eater of children, murderer of princesses but—lucky Michael—inclined to help the occasional itinerant idiot.

Second painting. *The Unsmiling Princess*. A masterpiece that sneaks up on you; in it, Lulu is unmistakable. A tower-bound maiden, listless and bored. Surrounded by suitors who, so the story goes, vie to make her smile, make her laugh, claim her hand. Twenty or more distinct faces of these men, each vivid in their individual expressions of mirth that little masks their scheming selfishness. Cajoling avarice. Wanton, foolish lust. These fleshy faces fill the canvas, surround the staid princess and leap from the canvas with an overwhelming sense of sin masked in humor.

In the story, this suitors' party of false merriment is a daily affair continuing for years.

Make my daughter smile, and her hand is yours.

And who is it, gets the unnamed princess to crack that smile? None other than the folkloric hayseed who, laboring in the fields, season in/season out, saves all his coins for a visit to the wonders of the city. (Nope, this guy never heard nothin' of a princess and her melancholia); fellow squanders his money, coin by coin, helping out strange insects and rodents—as Russian oafs are determined to do—along his way; he arrives in the capital penniless. Overwhelmed by the spectacle around the tower, abused by the crowds of men competing for the princess' smile, he slips and falls in the mud and dung. In trying to rise makes matters worse for himself, Laurel and Hardy *Muddled in Mud*, until his strange many-legged friends—especially the dung beetle—upright him in thanks for his kindnesses shown on his journey. The princess smiles, the king disapproves—the fellow is a halfwit—but the fool has captured whole his daughter's heart.

The Unsmiling Princess' dress was the giveaway. Clothed in an embroidered gown of white, its similarity to the evening dress Lulu wore at dinner was too exact.

Tuesday. Two paintings more. Michael Kingston arrived at Vasnetsov's house a changed man. It was obvious.

"A change has come over you, Mikhail Nikolaevich." *Michael Son of Nikoláj*, said the nutcracker with the pistol belt. And, "What have you done with the nervous, mad-eyed dog?" Grandma's Cookies remarked.

"What dog?"

"The one that lived inside you until today."

One of those nights.

Maybe the *night. Maybe I'm a little reborn this morning?*

Lovemaking with Lulu would always leave him feeling reborn afterward.

❦ ❦ ❦

AFTER MIDNIGHT, Lulu enters Michael's room. Slips, nude, beneath his sheets.

"It is my house. I come and go as I please."

"Is that a pun?"

His smile affirms it and it starts off exceptionally well.

"No. Stop. We're done."

"Not yet. I'd know."

"No jokes. Off me. Now." Pushes him. Hard.

Michael rolls onto his back. "You're a freak."

Her laughter delights Michael. She blankets his bare chest with her hair and nestles her head beneath his arm, beside his breast. "Tell me why I stopped."

"No earthly idea."

"I'm sorry. Did I ask your ego?"

"Why don't you go back to your bed?"

"He keeps speaking."

Michael grumbles. Lulu blows a puff of air at his cheek. "How do you know I don't love you?"

Odd phrasing. The real Michael, curious, answers. "How do I know you don't? Or how do I not know you do?"

"There you are. Yes. That is the riddle I meant."

"I'm not good at riddles."

"It doesn't need an answer. It only asks you to think."

"About whether you love me? Come on."

She strokes his chest. "You could replace the word 'love' in your thoughts with, I don't know? 'Sexually transmitted disease.'"

Michael laughs. "Okay. Fine. I was greedy. I wasn't thinking about you."

"Close."

"That's not it?"

"That's 'close.' You know what you were thinking about."

He props on his elbow. Stares at her. Alarmed. He does. "How would you know?"

"Because whether I love you—or not—Gwen doesn't belong in this bed with us."

"I didn't say her name."

"Lulu knows." She bats her eyes upward at his face. "A heart holding onto the wrong thing fucks wrong."

Michael stares. He's experienced nothing like Lulu before; as a Kingston he's never lain bare in truth.

She scoops away her hair as he rests back beside her. "My heart's not broken."

"No, Michael, it's not. Break it!" She pinched his triceps. Hard as she could.

"Ow!"

"It won't hurt this much. Break it. Let the pieces scatter. Sweep them up, and the pretend man you have made your whole life into being—" She opened her fingers. The pain dissipated. "Put him to rest. Be you. *Live."*

Lulu holds his face to her breasts for as long as it takes.

When he sleeps, she doesn't move. And when he wakes, she kisses him. Their lips nestle and fit and they breathe each other's air. Truly, he tells her; he has never kissed before. It made sense, as it resembled the revelation unveiled when the two of them, as one, made love.

"WHERE'S THE FROG?" said Michael.

"She is the frog. Hence the painting's title."

"*The Frog Princess.*"

Viewed dancing from behind, Vasnetsov's princess wears an embroidered emerald dress, a white shirt beneath, graceful and flowing, her head tilts back, her profile soft, her eyes shut, her happiness serene but undeniable. Arms extended, canted high and low, fingers curled and spread and lovely.

On the dance floor.

Hands supple. Fingers drooping. Undulating.

Leaves at the ends of lissome birch boughs in slow, soft, summer breeze.

A heart I wished my life for; it beats inside of her.

Two strong brothers; a third bumpkin. Dad says: fire arrows in three directions; where they land, you will find your bride. The youngest, the dumb one, finds his arrow held in the mouth of a frog. And so, of course, they are married. And, of course, beneath the frog skin, she is a wise and beautiful, magical princess. But only at night. Daytime: princess croaker. Once he discovers this, that her beauty is a different variety of "skin deep," he waits for his wife to transform and burns the frog skin.

"That doesn't go well for him, Mikhail Nikolaevich. Daylight reveals her in human form to the evil Kashchey."

Painting four.

"The old, bearded demon with the bloody broadsword holding her prisoner on his throne in a dungeon hall. She is as fair skinned as Ludmila."

"And the same eyes. The same color. Uncanny, isn't it? She stares at this one for hours. He is the Immortal One. The Deathless."

"You know who he looks like. Are you familiar with Goya?"

She smiled. "Yes. I see it. His eyes. His horror face. Saturn eating his own children. Both painted from the same nightmare, I imagine."

"Does the farm boy rescue her?"

"To kill Kashchey, one must destroy his heart, which he keeps hidden in the eye of a needle. The needle is inside an egg, inside a duck; the duck is inside a hare; that rabbit is inside a stone casket with the casket grown inside the top of the tallest oak tree."

Here it is: the mythology of Lulu's hidden heart.

"The village idiot gets his frog back?"

"His *wife*. With the help of various insects and animals, and fish he has befriended along the way. They knock down the tree. Smash the casket. Hunt and kill the animals—violent and bloody—crack the egg and snap! He breaks the needle, breaking the spell and slays the demon who has imprisoned her."

"My heart beats in one of these paintings... Even now, on the canvas..."

No second chance if you get your first chance wrong.

It's not Kashchey, which means it's not the Frog Princess...

The metaphor's too simplistic.

He scrutinized the docent's face. "We began with the Snow White of it all."

"It is Vasnetsov's masterpiece. More than *The Knight at the Crossroads.*"

His radar *pinged.*

She's adding information I didn't request.

"What's that? This knight. Another painting?"

A book retrieved. A catalogue for the State Russian Museum in St. Petersburg. A bookmarked page.

"*The Three Journeys of Ilya Muromets.* One of the other seven Fairy Tales."

A photograph of a gloomy canvas. A weary knight on a white horse, its mane and tail are long and thick and re-sembles Lulu's hair spread across his body as they loved in Michael's bed last night. Man and beast beaten by fatigue, insistent of an arduous trek. Vasnetsov depicts his worn hero from the side and behind. Reflection be-fore a stone inscribed with words. Michael squinted but couldn't make them out. Glagolitic alphabet, a precursor to modern Cyrillic.

"What's it say?"

"'If you go straight ahead, there will be no life; there is no way forward for he who travels past, walks past or flies past.'"

Michael chuckled. "He's going that way, though. So, sort of a riddle, huh?"

"It asks one to think."

A raven flies left. Others perch, watching, cawing at the chain and plate clad man. His scarlet spear aims down and right at scattered skulls and dry bones. The deathscape extends forever across the steppe.

"Did Lulu direct you to begin my study with *The Sleeping Tsarevna?*"

"Ludmila Igorevna suggested it would be a familiar story for you. Relax you to our folklore."

Michael walked up to the painting.

Along with the princess who sleeps upon the carved stone table in her fantasy garden—disregarding, for a moment, the slumbering doves and swans, the bear, the trustful rabbit snuggled up beside the peaceful fox—eight attendant maidens, two armed guards, a grandmother and grandfather, a trio of minstrels, dancers: all fast asleep at the moment the spell was cast. The most prominent figure—position/dimension-wise, Michael realized, was not the dramatic and most artistically detailed princess. No. It was the young, barefoot girl fallen asleep across the pages of a great book. Her lips still open from reciting; her finger still on the verse of ancient script.

"What's the book?"

"*The Book of the Dove*. Alina was seven when Lulu began her visits."

"Today?"

The old woman's gaze burned into Michael. "She would be fourteen."

"And *The Book of the Dove?* What's that?"

"A series of riddles King David answered to explain the origin of light, the sun, the moon, space. The energy of God. The most potent energy on the planet. Peace."

In his imagination, Michael leaped onto the back of his horse to gallop back to Lulu. In Moscow, he skipped the rush hour of the Metro. Bought himself a cab ride—she'd replenished his wallet; he squirmed at the thought of being her gigolo—but when her penthouse door opened, the younger bodyguard who itched to break his legs was the only person who remained.

"She's gone."

"Where?"

"*Chasovnya Opasnaya.*"

"Chapel Perilous? Her nightclub?"

"Chapel Perilous, the lady and Maxim's dacha. I am to drive you there if you are prepared to answer her question."

Michael nodded. He was. The bodyguard handed him a motorcycle helmet.

"You gotta be shitting me."

The bodyguard laughed, his English good enough for that. Jerked his head. "Come on, *amerikanski.*"

2.

ABOUT SEVEN MILES NORTH of Atmore, along Alabama Highway 21, the Fountain Correctional Facility emphasized rehabilitation in agriculture, vegetable gardening, cattle farming. Boone spent his seven-year bid working cotton. What drinking turpentine and wormwood stole of his sanity, extreme heat and humidity, bent over back-break and the glove/hand-shredding of the boll bracts, dust, dust, dust and the deliberate lack of modern machinery took the rest.

A taxi among half a dozen private vehicles. A short bus to run the unwanted or supervised-release halfway house bound into town. Melody leaned against the rear door of the cab and watched the wretched parade of free men and parolees belled out with their personal item garbage sacks, paperwork envelopes, expressions of joy, confusion, stubbornness of unrepentant hearts. As they separated—those to the bus, those that were free—guards gave a signal to family/friends. Some filtered forward. Greetings. Some cried honest joy. Others waited in their cars, hunched, braced, surrendered to the inevitability of recidivism.

Cab driver. Ran down the passenger window. "Wanna go meet 'im, I won' leave you, ma'am."

"Thank you. I'm just here to look."

No way he could have heard her, but Boone Kelso flashed eyes at his daughter as if called. He'd lost weight; years and weather had leathered his skin. He was shorter than she remembered, and maybe he'd lost an inch or two, but in the way the top of a stake loses that top inch to the pounding of a sledgehammer, compacting/hardening that wood and firming it immovable from the earth it's been driven into. His teeth weren't good, and his spread lips weren't smiling, the expression he shot her; his jaw constantly ground below his cheeks as if he had rocks in his mouth and enjoyed them the way other men enjoy tobacco.

He stopped. She didn't wave. He waited. She made him wait more.

"Move along Kelso, your bros wanna get to town."

He thrust his chin at her, like, *Well, girl?*

Melody nodded. Three times. *I've done it. I'm with you. I'm on your side.*

He did a thing with his thumb and forefinger, like a kid shaking a rootin'-tootin' cowboy gun. His tongue shot between his teeth like a snake and he laughed. Climbed onto the bus. It pulled forward. Curved around the lot. Passed by her. Boone Kelso visible in a window seat. Didn't look her way. Busy chatting, extra-animated, but no more than the ex-con beside him. Just two normal men getting away from abnormal life.

Back passenger side. Melody sat. Slumped relief.

"Friend? Family?"

"Father."

"I wouldn' a'done took him, he come over to the car. If I can say, you leave that man be."

"I appreciate your advice. I'm hoping to, once and for all. You can take me back now."

⚜ ⚜ ⚜

A ROOM AT THE ATMORE FAIRFIELD INN. Less than seventy dollars a night. Melody's second night; her same cab driver already booked for her morning ride to the Mobile airport. Rented bed sheets. Rented blanket. Rented air blown from the wall. Smug in the way it shoved that emptiness of place or care or meaning of circumstance in her face. Since she ordered pizza, she didn't think twice about opening the door at the polite tap-tap. Tap. from the other side. It wasn't the pizza guy. Sideswiped, Melody stepped back without thinking.

"How did you find me?"

Calvin Kirby of the Richmond, Virginia, District Attorney's office, opened his palms and lifted his shoulders in a "aw shucks" manner perfected by self-effacing men of the Old Dominion. Gotten him elected three terms in a row. He'd retire after this one.

"I thought you saw me when you watched him drive out."

"I didn't. How did you find me here?"

"Got lucky?" Lazy like a bobcat in a sunspot. But it wasn't sunny. Night and cold. No amount of cologne, of shirt starch, dimpled tie, and pressed three-piece suit made him as easy-going in person as he presented at a distance. Round face, round glasses, rounded gray hair and a roundabout manner.

"Couldn't let you go without checking in. You look like these eight years did you a lot of great with him put away."

"Mr. Kirby, you've come a long way to have the door shut in your face."

She shut it on him.

"Missus Kingston. You don't want him out any more than I." Ideal idea, talking through one-and-three-quarters of solid wood. "Just puzzles me why you won't help put him back in for as long as forever-amen for killing your mother."

The foot of her rented bed came level to Melody's eyes as she sunk to her haunches, her back against the door.

"Ma'am, something just holds you back from doing the right thing. The years churn and my calls and my letters keep going unanswered. Guy like Boone Kelso, what all he did, and knowing you know what-all whatever it is you do, might not think twice about doing it again."

She stared at her shaking hand. "You don't scare."

"No. You don't scare, but, ma'am, you were ten years-old whatever you think might give you some guilt holding back all these years. Mrs. Kingston, I will write up whatever agreement you want to keep you cozy as a kitten in your present life. All the bells and whistles that go along, ringing and tootin'."

My father rustles a Ziploc baggie. Seals the pistol inside.

"Pray, child, on your mama's murdered soul, you never see this again. It'll be what hangs you."

"Please leave."

"Please work with me. *Talk* to me. I want justice for both of you women. Christ's honor."

The sole of Mama's foot is the color of the top of my foot.

The top of her foot is the color of my eyes.
Except for the blood.

"I'll go now, Mrs. Kingston." His business card slipped beneath the door. She'd lost count how many she already had torn to pieces. "I am curious, though, how you end up married into the family of the last person he painted. Care to comment on that before I skedaddle?"

"What does that have to do with anything?"

"It's a pattern of something, isn't it?"

"My mother-in-law's portrait has nothing to do with my dead mother."

"I'm no detective. But when you've been doing what I've been doing long as I've been doing it, seeing what folks do one t'the other over stretches of time, you learn. Lean that there isn't a past. No more than there's a present or will ever be a future clean. It all hangs one thing, heavy like a black ball on a heavy black chain. That ball's solution ignores time. And unless you do something about that answer—past, present, future—it swings, and it wrecks its way through all three, knocking things down with indiscriminate and perfect accuracy. Bad day all around, so I feel for you. You have a pleasant flight home, Mrs. Kingston. A safe Thanksgiving."

Wednesday, November Twenty-first

N IGHT AND FRIGID. ICE crystals blowing, needles sharp against his face. Lulu's Skhodnya dacha, thirty-five kilometers northwest of Moscow. Forest side of the river. Arrived in darkness after a brutal ride on the back of the—Michael was sure of it—*psychotic* younger bodyguard's motorcycle. Frozen, Michael zeroed on the raging fireplace in the main salon, that burned in pieces every piece of an entire larch. At Foxtail Farm, Michael, his siblings, playmates, had all, one time, or another, ducked beneath the common room mantel to hide-and-seek inside the firebox; at Chapel Perilous three of four adults could have a cocktail party inside this fireplace. Or one big Guenever execution pyre with Lancelot riding inside to rescue her. Well, maybe not *that* large, but yes to the cocktail party and he hoped, as he shivered his way toward it, there would be some vodka to heat his insides while he toasted his skin without.

Not to be.

"This way, Mikhail Nikolaevich." Lulu's Chechen.

Can't call me Michael. Just has to goad me. And great, he's bundled up.

The Chechen led Michael into the sting of the wind; the needles now ice dendrites like ninja stars. They trudged a slippery path off the back deck and onto a forgotten lane. They reached the corner of a high stone wall, rough with hoarfrost. An ancient arch. Big curlicue hinges bent and rusted; the gate long gone. Beyond, an Orthodox chapel. Constructed of interlaced wooden planks and shingles. A single dome, broad metal, and rusted. Abandoned around the time of the Revolution. Little cared for since. Broken doors hung from larger versions of the gate hinges. One swung in the wind. All that was left to call it home. The Chechen pointed Michael through the tumbled graves about the chapel. Around the corner. Gave a little push.

"I don't know where I'm going."

"I don't think you'll get lost."

And he didn't. Halfway around the back, Lulu called, "Michael? You're here?"

"It's me."

She switched on a flashlight and guided him through the accumulating hoarfrost and dendritic snow. He joined her. She switched off her light.

It felt natural to embrace and kiss.

"If you'd taken any longer, we wouldn't be able to see. Even with the light."

"Switch it back on. Tell me what you want me to look at. Because this is serious cold out here."

"You have winter like this where you're from."

"You would think. All I can say is Russian cold is tooth socket cold. I have never experienced that before. The holes my teeth sit in hurt."

She stroked his face with her mitten. Left her hand upon his frozen cheek. "You found my heart. Yes?"

Michael pressed against the warmth coming through from her hand. He nodded. "You are each of Vasnetsov's princesses and they each tell a portion of your story. This isn't my guess, but Kashchey is Kolya?"

She imprisoned the answer she wanted to give him behind a tight, thin smile. "Tell me. My heart."

"Is the girl with the book. Your daughter. Alina."

"Alina is my heart."

"I'm sorry, what's happened to you."

Lulu switched on her flashlight. Aimed its beam at the ground off the path a short distance before them.

Three graves. She said, "That is Maxim's. He is there."

She leaned into Michael. He reached across her back. She let him pull her against him.

She said, "That is mine."

"You're here."

Again, the smile, tight smile. Perfect six-point snowflakes, hard like confectioner's sugar, decorative and unique, the way children are told and imagine all snowflakes appear but rarely ever see. She aimed her light at the last grave and Michael held her tight.

He said, "That's your Alina."

"Her grave, but she is in Germany. An academy. I am allowed to visit her twice a year. Summer and Christmas. Because Uncle Kolya would not let them kill me, they have made my daughter my jailer."

"Why? What could you possibly do to...?"

"My husband's partners; Putin's oligarchs? Me? Nothing. Alina and I are just leverage against Kalaydoskop.

They were unhappy Kolya cut them out of the Gazprom pipeline."

"Nord Stream."

"Nord Stream One. They are fighting over control and purpose of a much larger Nord Stream Two. That is where my father was sending you. To the negotiation. Where you would meet your father. In Baku. The oil conference. Pinwheel, as you knew him, as your 'dad' knew him, gave me everything you need to get you in, through security and undercover, onto our Russian team."

"Why would he/they want me there—part of a Russian espionage operation?"

"All I know is I have what you need if you want to go."

"I can fuck it all up for them. That *is* what I'd do."

"Then do it! You understand: no one—from any country—appears that concerned with stopping you. Preventing you from doing anything."

"When is this oil conference?"

"The week between Christmas and New Year's."

The snow was falling fast and heavy. The graves disappearing.

"What do you want me to do?"

"About Kalaydoskop? Why ask me?"

"No. I'm going to do that. You said there was a trade."

She shouldered out of his grip. Extinguished the light and tucked its metal tube beneath her arm. She took both of his hands. "In exchange for the documents you need—credentials, your cover—you will free my daughter and deliver her to me."

You're going to lose her. You're already losing her.

"I must face him."

Kalaydoskop. Kolya. Father.

"I swear—I pledge to you—I will come back to you."

"No. You could come with us. But once you've saved me, given me my Alina, we will vanish. Where she and I go, no one will find us."

"Why can't I have both?"

"Because this—me—my offer, is real life. There is no cover you can play someone else, create massive complications for others, and walk back to something else and call it 'clean' and call that 'yourself.'"

"I don't know what that means."

She grabbed his sleeve. Tugged him, follow. "We have time to figure it out." She led him back around the church. "I think we'll stay here for a while. You can teach me about your Thanksgiving holiday. And I can teach you—"

"About love?"

Lulu found the funny in that. "That would be rather stupid."

"That hurts."

"Not you. Because I would end up falling and you would have already landed. By then, you will have left me."

Thursday, November Twenty-second – Thanksgiving

1.

*D*REXLER; *LAST WEEK.* "*HOUTEN and his hotshots are snobs. Contractors who contract out their quartermaster services. You'll rotate in to baste the turkey and mix up the green whipped cream pineapple and pecan shit.*"

"*And serving him and his boys will somehow get him to take a shine to me?*"

"*Nope. You'll have this shine to lend a hand.*" *He slapped down a set of prisoner photos.*

"*Got your racial slurs wrong, fatman.*"

"*Just memorize his face. We'll do some run-throughs the rest of this week. I'll give you a night with your wife and off you'll go.*"

AT CAMP ABU OMAR in the Kurdistan Region of Iraq, it was already Thanksgiving Day. Windy and cool. Mojtaba Niavarani knew nothing of the meaning behind the American holiday. If it was holy to their infidel god, so be it; it made his task less complicated. His thankfulness to Allah, Glory be to Him, the Exalted, filled his heart as he made his way, unaccosted, through blowing sand to the American mess where scheduling/duty adjustments allowed two hours for most US personnel and the privileged of their Sunni lap dogs to gather for their celebratory meal.

Truly, God is great. Within the space of two weeks, His divine hand opened the way for Mojtaba. Four years after his capture with his Iranian brethren serving the Mahdi's Army against the multinational force, someone mistakenly identified him as a Sunni fighter. Mistaken incarceration. Pulled from hell and transferred to a hospital. A week of rest/recuperation. A pair of Americans presented him with an offer to train with a force of Jundallah fighters; a Sunni Salafi militant organization known as the People's Resistance Movement of Iran (PRMI). Scum.

Last night, Allah's Will, his guiding hand, once more provided for Mojtaba. Beneath his field jacket, he wore the claymore mine he'd stolen with miraculous ease. Allah be praised.

He entered the mess without incident. He cast out his pride with prayer at the ease with which all gates flung wide for him. He guessed there were forty men, including kitchen staff. Mojtaba would collect a tray. Receive his food. Conceal the M57 Electrical Firing Device underneath his tray and, within ten minutes, send the infidels to hell as he joined his brothers in paradise.

Mojtaba Niavarani was not incorrect that all he'd done was under a guiding hand. But the hand didn't belong to Allah. It was fat and resembled a pink hydrangea.

Mojtaba collected his tray and moved in line along the serving counter.

♛ ♛ ♛

SUPER 8/ROUTE 235/LEXINGTON PARK. Fergus pounded on Clive's door until he opened it. Six in the morning. Clive only in bed since two. Answered the door in his bed-sheet.

"What?"

"Where's the brandy?"

Clive rubbed his face. "It's cognac, you wanker."

"It's a party today." Fergus's breath reeked of the IPA party he'd already started late in the night, scanning frequencies and listening to dead air as he'd done for a month. "You're going to make sure old Silas serves it."

"And if he doesn't?"

"Break into that cellar. Tonight."

"When/if he discovers that?"

"Bollocks. You stole wine; got his underage grand-daughter pissed for the holiday."

Breathing hard. Exhausted. Dying to get back to bed. "You're pissed and full of bad ideas, and I'm going back to sleep."

Fergus tried to grab him. Came away with the sheet. Got an eyeful. "*That* keeps her happy?"

Drunk Fergus always wanted a fight.

"Take a running jump, Fergie." Snatched back the sheet. Didn't have the energy to re-wrap. "I just finished the map last week."

"As it turns out, no different from the original plans."

"Got every stick of furniture. So you don't bloody trip over yourself when you get the balls to go inside yourself."

"That map is not for me, brother." He raised a hand like he was going to toss a slap. Patted Clive's cheek. "The Timeless. Not my order. Comes from Legoland. Tonight."

♛ ♛ ♛

SILAS KINGSTON'S LAPTOP alerted when Fergus left Garde-Joyeuse. The slob hadn't gone out in ten days. Silas went down to the North Vista wine cellar. Damp and cold and cobwebbed. The air thick with dust. Down the center aisle between dusty shelves of cased wine and single, dusty bottles. Stopped at the empty crate. Dug the two bent framing nails from the straw at the bottom. Crouched. Nails into wall holes. Wrist twist and a practiced pull, false panel removed. Withdrew the grimy box with his radio transceiver and scuffed Russian code book.

Back inside the North Vista Outhouse; carried the radio up to the attic. On a table, he removed the transceiver's case. He replaced the original crystals with the pair he smuggled out of headquarters. This would change the operating frequency of the device. As the crystals act as a precise frequency reference for the oscillator circuit within, swapping the crystals would result in different frequency transmission and reception frequencies than previously broadcast. Onto the widow's walk, he ran the antenna wire back through the glass door, into the attic, into his radio reassembled. Silas activated his radio and set it to scanning the new channels. Angry, impotent, bored, and drunk, Fergus would take some time to stumble upon his open signal.

He left his quarters. On the lawn, he checked the weather. Cold, humid, thick clouds scattered beneath the setting moon like running gray cavalry charging past overhead. The clouds over the river bay—blacker, heavier, sluggish. They were the artillery. In time, would press in on Foxtail Farm, lower their barrels in the sky to thunder on the Kingstons throughout the afternoon.

Storms; always good for holidays in winter. Good for fires. Good for warm and fragrant kitchens. Good for closing out the world; forcing families close.

Silas crossed the lawn to the manor porch. Up the steps. Inside. Treading softly. He looked for Beaumont inside his crate. Crate open, Claypoole hound, gone. Donut bed removed.

He lowered his voice. "Beaumont!" Nothing. Repeated calls louder. Snapped finger emphasis. Tinkle of the dog's collar.

Silas found Beaumont on his dog bed beneath Doris's portrait and he heard, plain as if she stood behind him, *"In 1904, a thunderstorm gathered over Tula. The blackest storm anyone had ever seen."*

"You share the same majesty, my dear."

A little voice responded, "She says a storm's coming." Tangled, sleep-haired/sleep-faced Leigh peered over the top rail. Faint char where Doris went over.

"Did you bring his dog bed here?"

A dramatic shrug. "He did it himself. I guess."

"Get your robe and some outside slippers."

"My Crocs?"

"Those stupid things, yes. Come walk Beaumont with me."

"It's still dark."

"That makes it an adventure."

Delight. She scampered for robe and shoes and down-stairs she whirled.

As they went outside, Silas said, "I'll tell you some-thing you don't know. And it's true."

"About Gramma Doris?"

Intuitive. Just like her mother. Lynn, he thought and saddened. Put on a smile. "That's right. Your grandmoth-er came to me from the inside of a storm."

"Was it a tornado? Like Dorothy? I had a dream about that, once. Oooh! It's cold. Wait. I want a hat."

When she returned and she said, "Oh, and Hap-py Thanksgiving." Silas responded in kind and they went out, grandfather, granddaughter, dog bouncing be-tween, and Silas forgot to ask about her dream.

♕♕♕

No matter where you are in the world, as an Ameri-can gathered with other Americans, even Americans you don't know, gratefulness for a meal shared for a common purpose of gratitude—even if the work you're doing, work you believe in, has thrust you into a hellhole desert filled with nothing you love and most of the things you hate—there's a peace that radiates from all that is good that God/the US Army has provided you. Provided for your family you are away from. Your communal meal not only connects all of you, present and clumped together in sameness in your mess, but each of your homes and family, loved ones and friends, in multitudinous variation, shared privacies, it draws you together, away a moment from the grueling shit work you're doing. All those private lives—at least for this shared hour—glow as one inside the drab and impersonal tent Thanksgiving Day.

Hal knew it. Felt gratitude. Carved turkey. Double-tined fork and poultry knife—a carver with a shorter blade and a more articulated point for working with smaller-boned meat.

Mojtaba Niavarani didn't know. He was thankful, sure, but only for what he would deliver. Death. Once he walked with his Thanksgiving meal to the center of the tent.

The American asked if he was having meat.

"Please. Yes."

Hal watched Mojtaba shift his right hand into and out of the folds of his jacket. Didn't need to see the clacker. He waited until Mojtaba's forearm turned palm-side up. Drove his carving fork through the tray, pinning Mojtaba's hand/arm in place, sabering down and through the Iranian's forearm with the poultry carver.

Mojtaba Niavarani's scream filled the mess hall, but the message from his brain to his hand never reached his fingers, stopped at the severed ends of his flexor tendons.

The absolute silence of the instant of attack. Before shouts/cries/Hal tackled, a look passed between the two men. Knowledge of the set-up between them. Hal couldn't afford that story coming out and his knife flashed once more, cutting the throat of the terrorist who fell back in gouts of blood.

☫ ☫ ☫

THE SPA AND SALON at the Four Seasons Georgetown, D. C., did a half-day Thanksgiving and Lynn booked Layla Kingsbury a facial, hair, and nails. Lent Roman her car for tennis with Aydin.

Aydin was off his game. Quiet, worried about Elmin's recent and distinct emotional distance. Didn't play his best. Roman won the first set. They took some light refreshment at the juice bar. Roman asked if Aydin thought Elmin was cheating.

"It's not. It's not that. Guy's getting a taste of extra become more sexually aggressive with their own man. Not less. It's like a high and you crave more and more. At least that's my experience." He tried a wink. There was nothing behind it. He hurt. "I know you can't discuss it, but is it something at work? Something political?"

"Not that I know. Honestly, he slow-walked my promotion. But, you know, he knows I'm not the most qualified. Favor to you, favor to my dad's memory. Didn't go slow with Layla, though. Maybe his wife's coming in."

"He'd have told me. Maybe it's his time of the month."

Roman rolled his eyes. "I'll feel him out tonight."

"Oh, yeah, Layla gonna like that."

"Aydin, you're gross."

"And you're lucky with her."

"I am. Thank you." Roman fist bumped his cousin.

They played another set. He didn't let Aydin get a point. On his way out, a pretty employee he didn't recognize, asked if he'd like the calendar the club, this year, was handing out as a holiday gift. He thanked her. Glanced at it. Typical historical pictures of the club, its member highlights/tournaments/parties through the years. Brought it with him to Layla's car.

♛ ♛ ♛

CONFINED TO QUARTERS. Under armed guard. Unsung, but altogether hero of Camp Abu Omar, Hal came to attention at the entrance of Finn Houten.

"Happy Thanksgiving, corporal."

"Yes, sir. Happy Thanksgiving, sir."

"May I ask you a serious question, corporal?"

"Yes, sir, Mister Houten, sir."

"What the fuck?"

"Sir?"

"If this were regular army, you'd be up for a medal."

"May I speak freely, Mr. Houten, sir?"

"I am."

"Fuck medals. I saw a need. I filled it."

Houten called. "Sergeant, remove Corporal Cooper's restraints."

Hal's guard executed the order as Houten: "You weren't always with the quartermasters?"

"Prior service was not with the Army, sir. Have some familiarity with what an M57 looks like in Ali Baba's hands."

Houten studied Hal. "The investigation should go quick. You and I will talk after that. Till then—anything you need."

"Yes, sir."

Houten staring hard. Weighed, measured, liked what he saw. "Anything you want to tell me before I go digging around on you, corporal?"

"All of it's true. Even the half that wasn't writ' down."

GWEN HAD REARED HER HEAD; would arrive just in time for dinner. Unsurprising. With her and the girls; counting herself and the twins; Silas, no Lynn, but add Clive: nine. But the twins count for one, so Melody prepared Foxtail Farm Thanksgiving for eight. Ten-pound bird for eight adults would leave plenty for her hand-shredded leftover turkey with cranberry sauce mayo sandwiches which, because there wasn't one of them who didn't love the sourdough loaves she baked, made the holiday last all weekend.

Two kinds of potatoes—mashed and sweet-baked with marshmallow. Stuffing. Green beans with shallots, garlic, and thyme. Two kinds of pies—pumpkin and chocolate pecan. Each of Gwen's girls helped. Clive came over, tried to pitch in until Paige threw him out. Silas, on the porch, ignored him. Beaumont whined for a while, lamenting the rain, then pretzel'd in front of the dining room fire and slept. Clive watched football; ever since *Friday Night Lights*, it had grown on him.

The morning swept by, early afternoon right behind, on a series of kitchen timers.

"I'm going up to dress." Paige.

"Girls, you go with her. Jack, Little Silas, we'll do us-three in a minute, once I get these pies in."

"Did I need to bring a jacket?" Clive.

Silas. "She said 'dress.' If you've brought one of those, feel free to put it on." He returned his attention to Doris's White book, making notations only he understood on a yellow pad.

Clive watched the rain. Said, "I could brave the storm and bring up some wine."

Silas. "Already have."

Gwen arrived, puddling and sparking like a wet wire. Sparking with dangerous energy. That energy increased when Paige came down to table in Doris's red dress. Silas's smile was all teeth. And Leigh, who was experimenting with long velvet ribbons, said, "I'm glad you're wearing it."

"Honey, I am too," Gwen purred. "So much meaning to this family."

Silas folded his hands. "Clive, since you got out of all the work, you ask the blessing."

"Papa!" Paige put her hand on Clive's. "I'll do it. You don't have to."

"I got this. Um, this is one we said in my house. 'God is good, God is great and we thank him'— Oh, cripes. Switched it backwards— 'for our/this plate.'"

Leigh giggled.

Charlotte observed, "I like it better. 'good' and 'food' never rhymed."

Paige kissed him.

They feasted. Outside, the storm intensified, and Beaumont howled at the thunder. Everyone agreed he wasn't afraid but was standing guard. Confronting it. Leigh asked Papa to tell the story about how Gramma Doris came from a storm.

He surprised them all with the story of "Indiana's Miracle"—except for Melody, who always expecting the best from him; felt only a warmth of pride and heard in the love he hid behind his words, her husband's voice.

"When we returned home with your dad—"

Charlotte shook her head. "I can't even picture him as a baby."

"I gave her the first Beaumont."

"It would be the second," Leigh corrected. "Because she lost her first one in the tornado. What happened to your Beaumont? Did Daddy play with it?"

Gwen, who hadn't been listening, finished the wine in her glass. Poured more. Then, as if toasting, interrupted. "Let's finish up, girls. You're coming home with me tonight."

Charlotte groaned. Leigh froze. Paige looked at Clive before saying, "Good luck with that. I'm not going anywhere with you."

"God dammit, Paige. I am still your mother."

"Watch it," Silas snapped. "Paige is an adult. And if you get behind the wheel of a car in this storm after all you've had to drink, you'll be losing in court on a DUI rather than losing to me with your flyspeck suit."

Gwen buttoned her lip; her lawyers would advise she not say another word. Instead, she vomited every word she could remember of Senator Ossani strategizing with her before bursting into tears and fleeing upstairs.

Paige shouted after her. "Don't go in my room!"

Melody. "Take mine! Freshen up! I'll make you some tea!" Exasperated eyes: "Silas."

"Oh, gobble-gobble." He looked at everyone. Ended on Clive. "Fancy an after-dinner drink?"

👑👑👑

DRESSED. MAKE-UP IN PLACE. Waiting for Roman's text, Lynn burned anxiety with half her bangle flask. She topped it off and threw away the empty bottle. Admired herself in the standing mirror of the room he rented for her. For them. For later. A spiced-cinnamon boucle bead Teri Jon cocktail dress; half-sleeves and crew neckline rough-edged/fringed. Hoped Roman would like it. Her. Her-with-him.

Not what this is about, girl.

Azerbaijan Revival Day; Gary already has OTS falsifying proof Roman's father was murdered by the Soviets. Everything's happening. Working to operation. So why do I feel gutless and horrible?

Text dinged in. **"Be there 5 min."**

Out lobby/out doors. He pulled up in front of her.

"Perfect timing," she said as he got out and came around. Opened her door. Snug inside beside him, she complimented his gray unstructured suit. He leaned over and kissed her, and she caressed his face.

"A girl could cut herself on that jaw, mister."

He drove. Light rain. Auto-wipers, silent swish. V-8 hammering to be set free.

"How was tennis?"

"Not bad."

"You win?"

Nodded. Focused on the road ahead.

"You seem quiet."

"Relishing in your kiss. Layla. If that's not love, I don't know..."

Lynn's skin prickled. Light laugh. "Let's not get ahead of ourselves on our first official night out."

"Is this official, Lynn? I mean, it must be."

Another airy laugh.

Keep cool.

"You called me 'Lynn.' How'd you find out?"He took the rolled calendar from the door pocket. "April." Wouldn't look at her.

And there it was. Spring mixer, 2006. Post tournament. Group photo; loser in the back; names along the bottom.

You got this, Layla. Come on, girlfriend.

"April Fools?" The rain came harder. The wipers picked up the pace. The engine hammered. "I guess *that* was the deception the lie detector didn't catch. I changed my name after the divorce."

Salvage, salvage, salvage.

Hand on his thigh.

He's burning up.

Hyper-aware of her bangle touching the side of his leg. He didn't touch her.

"Everyone's got a job." Glanced at her. "In a weird way, we work in the same business. The lengths you went to should flatter me."

Say nothing. You've done the work. Bound to happen. Sovs murdered his father. That's the program. Let him inch back to you.

"Do you have any feelings for me at all?"

Lie. Lie. Lie.

"No."

Saw him face her from the corner of her eye. She stared at the rain.

"That's not what I expected. Which of you is lying?"

Lynn. It's all I know. I'm fucked up.

"Roman, I can't do this. Pull over. Let me out."

"There's nowhere. It's raining. I'm in your car."

"Damn right it's my car! Do it!"

"I want to settle something. Who kisses me the way you kiss me?"

"You know I'm pretending. Now pull over!"

"Who? Layla or Lynn?"

Fire in her eyes. "Lynn. Layla was doing just fine. Lynn's the motherfucker who kissed you like—God, I'm trying to save your ass!"

He laughed at her. Shook his head. "Lynn: if Layla doesn't show up with me—you vanish? You've destroyed me."

"You found out so easily. I come with you and when they find out—that's treason for you." She peered through the rain. "We're getting close. Slow down. Please."

Why is it you're breaking my heart?

"If I hadn't found out. And you'd found the right moment and asked. Could have even been tonight. I would have helped you. I hate my job. Leashed back to the Russians."

He pulled to the embassy gates. A quick peek by the guard. He drove inside. The driveway looped around the business side to a private/formal entrance. A valet with an umbrella stepped forward, then paused as Lynn leaned in; she buried her fingers in his hair and kissed him again. Fire and passion and truth.

"That was Lynn. That was all me."

A quick look in the mirror. Out. Up the three stone steps. Roman opened the door for her and they entered together. They stopped inside the receiving room. The only guests. Elmin on a settee. Palpable fury. A coffee table. The Rock Creek Tennis Club Holiday calendar lay open to April in the center of the table.

Two security officers bracketed Roman. Jackets tucked behind their holsters. Grabbed Roman's arms at his elbows. Roman braced.

Elmin said, "Resistance will only make this worse for you, Roman... Ms. Kingston, please have a seat."

2.

CLIVE ROSE FROM HIS chair. "Sounds great, Silas. Tell me what you want, I'll go fight the rain for it."

Silas pushed from the table, fished keys from his pocket. "Melody. You've been down there. It's cognac. It's called Timeless, you've seen the bottle. Second row. Halfway down. Top shelf. It was a gift, you know."

Clive glanced suspicion at Paige. Pushing to her feet, looking past him. Outside. Into the rain. A strobe of red and blue light. "Papa, there's police or an ambulance at the gate. You think Mom called the cops?"

"She wouldn't..." Silas, off guard, didn't like it. The gate buzzer sounded. "Melody, open the gate." He hurried into the rain.

♕ ♕ ♕

GWEN WRESTLED Charlotte and Leigh's carry-on/rollers outside. Noticed the police cruiser. Silas under Melody's umbrella at the driver's window.

Ha! Hope they arrest the old kook!

"Charlotte! Leigh! My car, now!"

"Don't you drive! Girls, don't go with her." Silas.

"Shut up, old man."

"Mom?" Leigh.

"Girls, get in the car. Paige—this isn't over between us."

"Drive safe, Mom. Charlotte, I'll call you. Look out for your sister."

Silas: "I said, you're not leaving."

"Papa: let her."

Paige seemed to placate him. Gwen and the girls hustled through the rain to her car.

A man sat in the back seat of the police car.

"What is this about, officer?" Silas said. "Who's that with you?"

"It's a welfare check, sir. Sorry, to disturb your holiday. Everything alright with her?" The cop cocked his head in Gwen's direction.

"Yes. She just suffers from idiocy. They'll be fine."

"Papa, I know who he is. Mr. Kirby?" The back window slid down.

"I've been trying to reach you."

"I blocked your number."

"And I've missed my Thanksgiving because of it."

Melody faced Silas under their shared umbrella. "He's the DA out of Richmond."

Silas stepped back. "I'll let you have some privacy." Already looking around. Paige and Clive gone.

"What do you want, Mr. Kirby?"

"What I want is your cooperation. More, now that Boone Kelso broke out of his electronic monitoring device and escaped his supervised release. I think it's likely he'll be coming here, don't you?"

"I don't know—"

Silas: "Paige? Clive?"

"—I don't care. But okay, I'll call you if he shows up and you can arrest him again. Problem solved." Melody moved back to the patrol officer's window. "Anything else we can do, sir?"

The police officer shifted his gaze to his rearview. Calvin Kirby shook his head.

♛ ♛ ♛

THE CASE OF TIMELESS on the floor. Clive snapping photos of their labels, the serial numbers with his phone.

Paige, a stranger to this place, uncomfortable with their activities, explored unsettled and aimless. "Would you hurry?"

"You could help."

"I got a pit in my stomach. Nothing's right. I can't believe my mom. And the cops with Melody—what was that all about?"

"I'm almost done." He snapped the last two. Packed the case.

"Hey, this is weird…"

Above. Outside. "Paige? Clive, you down here?" The door.

Paige at the back wall. A panel. Size of a playhouse door. Opened. "Clive, you're going to like this." She tugged it open. Dark inside. "I found a secret room. I swear to God."

Clive shoved his phone in his pocket. Hoisted the case back to the shelf.

Silas. Descending the stairs. Into view, seeing Clive, turning, holding up the cognac.

"This is the one, right?"

"You bet." He steers past Clive, craning his neck, moving toward the back. "Paige!"

Paige screamed. Clive and Silas rushed. Horror led, filling Paige's face, emerging from the secret room.

"...papa...?"

Grandfather/granddaughter frozen in/by the moment. The earth lurched between them. Clive tried to push inside. Paige fought him back. "It's horrible. Never look in there."

"Inward Light." Melody moving down the dusty aisle.

Wooden ships.

Black iron chains.

The sole of Mama's foot is the color of the top of my foot. Except for the blood.

"The Place of Blackness."

Silas kept focus on Paige. "That's correct. It's a torture chamber."

"Why do we have it?" Paige can't unsee it.

"It's always been here."

Melody said, "Your ancestors tortured and murdered slaves in there."

"Are you serious?" Clive forward, ducked in the doorway.

"Let him look."

"No, Papa!" Paige pushed Clive back.

Melody faced Silas. "Why you wanted me to fetch the bottle. Me, not them. You knew. You left it open for me to find."

Paige's eyes. Accusing. Betrayed. Melody. "You knew this place was here? *You. Knew?*"

Flash! Calvin Kirby. "Past, present, future... It swings, and it wrecks its way through all three, knocking things down with indiscriminate and perfect accuracy."

Melody centered. "It's the history of our family. Ours to defend."

3.

"**Y**OU ARE A DESPICABLE, filthy whore."

"I'm an employee of the US Federal Government, host nation to your embassy. The next step is a call to the DSS."

"Don't dictate terms to me, *fahişə!*" *Slut/harlot/prostitute!*

I'm sure that's lovely. At least we're in his office. Cool head.

"The Diplomatic Security Service is the primary law enforcement agency that investigates crimes in foreign embassies in the United States. Because I am an invited guest, I've not committed any crime except falsifying identification. There isn't very much except PNG'ing me, that you can do. However, before they arrive, the three-letter agency I work for would be very interested in seeing no harm come to Mr. Roman Sayadov."

"You got balls!"

"And you like to put yours inside men's mouths. We can make this extremely beneficial. Not only for you personally, but for your nation. A trade of some kind, in this situation, is not unheard of."

It's in his eyes. I got him.

A commotion. Door thrown wide. Lynn and Elmin startled/called "Roman?!"

Roughed up. Wild-eyed. Gun at the temple of one of the security officers. "Lynn: up. We're going."

"Roman, no. Surrender the weapon, right now. There's an easier way."

"Listen to your slut. I can make a deal. *Aydin* wouldn't want anything to happen to you."

Listen to him. Hear what's he's saying.

"Fuck that! Lynn, come right now." He pressed the barrel hard into the officer's ear.

"Okay-okay." Lynn raised her hands. A desperate look at Elmin. She joined Roman in the doorway.

Made it to the reception room. To the door.

"Open it, Lynn."

"Roman: it becomes a serious crime once you step through that door with that man."

"They won't do anything."

He reached for the handle. Levered it and the second security proved him wrong with a single shot. Roman's head slammed against the door. He collapsed.

Lynn staggered. Saw he was dead. Felt his misplaced—

(but right placed; God: I did this)

—love rise past her. She fell to her knees where miracles weren't happening. CPR useless to a hole in the head.

"You didn't have to kill him." Lynn choked. The scar tissue inside her throat constricted.

The security officer grabbed his gun. Elmin held out his hand. For the other gun.

"We didn't. You did." He signaled the man who took the shot. "Lock her up. I'll contact the authorities. We will handle the investigation in-house, as is our diplomatic right."

4.

T HE RAIN SHOWED NO sign of slackening and pounded at the leaded windows of the North Vista Outhouse attic, flung like gravel against the single swing-pane door. Harker's letter to Silas lay unopen at his elbow on the large map table where Silas watched Fergus scan his radio, drink his whisky, scratch his crotch. Silas worked the book code he'd fashioned that afternoon from *The Once and Future King*.

He applied the code to a letter he wrote. A letter that began:

May it please Your Majesty,

Truth has a way of rising no matter how deeply you bury it, and the demons never remain invisible. In order to avert what I fear will be a terrible loss of lives, I offer you my confession...

Movement on his computer screen. Fergus jolts upright. Peering, obsessed, a new signal on his monitoring equipment. A broadcast frequency he checks against pages inside his sloppy notebook. Doesn't find it.

Silas lifted the hand-mike.

"Kalaydoskop, Kalaydoskop. Cat's Eye to Kalaydoskop..."

No one to answer. Crystals calibrated to seek a long dead channel that, once Fergus reports it, will crackle to life many long ago suspicions. He taunted Fergus off and on for over an hour, putting the call into empty space, working on his confession, and at some point, Silas slept. Dreamed.

His finger pulls the trigger. The pistol fires. Evander Lott falls forward, his spit-flinging curses dying on his lips.

Smoke curls from the barrel of the gun.

Silas picks up the dog. Picks up Doris's Beaumont. Walks from Moscow to the porch at Foxtail Farm. Doris is there. Third step. Over to the right. Where Doris always sits. Waits.

"I heard a gunshot."

Silas nods. Returns Beaumont to her arms. Tail-wagging, all tongue, all exhausted. Embraces his young wife, the mother of their son, Michael.

"What if we never get what we deserve?"

"We give thanks—" Beaumont squiggles from her arms. Bounces around their feet— "for all the grace we do find, and hold, and keep."

He crushes himself to his wife, to his future, and whispers, "Our tornado balances inside a kaleidoscope."

About The Author

AWARD-WINNING NOVELIST MICHAEL FROST Beckner began a Hollywood career as writing assistant to Academy Award winner Barry Levinson on "Good Morning, Vietnam" and "Rain Man". In 1989, Beckner's script for "Sniper" launched a military-thriller franchise now on its eleventh sequel. Three consecutive record-breaking spec script sales and three films later, Tony Scott directed Beckner's original screenplay "Spy Game." An international hit that paired Robert Redford and Brad Pitt as CIA partners and rivals, it is now a classic in the espionage genre.

The pilot for Beckner's CIA-based television drama "The Agency" for CBS, predicted Osama bin Laden's terror attack and the War on Terror four months before 9/11. In that series alone, Beckner would go on to predict three more international terror events.

Having penned close to 100 original screenplays, adaptations, and teleplays in the employ of every major film studio, television network, and cable outlet, he is a Hollywood institution.

As a commentator on American espionage, Beckner has appeared on CNN, Fox News, CBS News, TF1 in France, and as a featured guest of Bill Maher on HBO.